A VOYAGE TO THE HELLHOLE OF SPACE

The Terrans wanted Basil Donovan for a long interstellar voyage into one of the most feared regions of outer space. They needed him to guide them into the Black Nebula—a place from which few starships had ever returned. But Donovan hated the Terrans. They had conquered his planet and turned his life as a member of the Royal Family into a shambles. However, there was more to it than just hating the Terrans. Donovan had been one of the few men to ever come back from the Black Nebula alive. And since his return, his grip upon his own sanity had been tenuous at best. He had been a captive in the Black Nebula, the captive of a race of bizarre alien creatures whose mental powers were far beyond those of ordinary human beings. There was also a beautiful female alien waiting for him there, a green-eyed alien whom he both hated and loved. And he knew she would never let him go home again—alive.

FOR A COMPLETE SECOND NOVEL, TURN TO PAGE 77

CAST OF CHARACTERS

BASIL DONOVAN

He was a stubborn, prideful member of the Royal Family of Ansa. But his Terran conquerors wanted him to guide them into the Black Nebula, a terrifying place he knew only too well.

HELENA JANSKY

She was the beautiful commander of a Terran spaceship. The contempt she felt for Donovan was magnified by the fact that he was leading them on what might well be a suicide mission.

VALDUMA

She possessed the heart and soul of Basil Donovan. The memory of her beauty and touch had captivated him for years. Unfortunately, she was also a crazed alien she-devil!

WOCHA

His looks were that of a misshapen monster. But he was fiercely loyal and stood ready to defend his master's life with his own.

TAKAHASHI

As Jansky's executive officer, his skill would be invaluable in navigating their ship through the depths of the Black Nebula.

MAROVECH

He was a laughing half-devil, whose words Donovan had so much enjoyed in earlier days. But now he came to slay him.

SARGASSO OF LOST STARSHIPS

By
POUL ANDERSON

ARMCHAIR FICTION
PO Box 4369, Medford, Oregon   97501-0168

*For more information about Armchair Books and products, visit our
website at…*

www.armchairfiction.com

Or email us at…

armchairfiction@yahoo.com

CHAPTER ONE

BASIL DONOVAN was drunk again. He sat near the open door of the Golden Planet, boots on the table, chair tilted back, one arm resting on the broad shoulder of Wocha, who sprawled on the floor beside him, the other hand clutching a tankard of ale. The tunic was open above his stained gray shirt, the battered cap was askew on his close-cropped blond hair, and his insignia—the stars of a captain and the silver leaves of an earl on Ansa—were tarnished. There was a deepening flush over his pale gaunt cheeks, and his eyes smoldered with an old rage.

Looking out across the cobbled street, he could see one of the tall, half-timbered houses of Lanstead. It had somehow survived the space bombardment, though its neighbors were rubble, but the tile roof was clumsily patched and there was oiled paper across the broken plastic of the windows. An anachronism, looming over the great bulldozer that was clearing the wreckage next door. The workmen there were mostly Ansans, big men in ragged clothes, but a well-dressed Terran was bossing the job. Donovan cursed wearily and lifted his tankard again.

The long, smoky-raftered taproom was full—stolid burgers and peasants or Lanstead, discharged spacemen still in their worn uniforms, a couple of tailed greenies from the neighbor planet Shalmu. Talk was low and spiritless, and the smoke that drifted from pipes and cigarettes was bitter, cheap tobacco and dried bark. The smell of defeat was thick in the tavern.

"May I sit here, sir? The other places are full."

Donovan glanced up. It was a young fellow, peasant written over his sunburned face in spite of the gray uniform and the empty sleeve. Olman—yes, Sam Olman, whose family had been under Donovan fief these two hundred years. "Sure, make yourself at home."

"Thank you, sir. I came in to get some supplies, thought I'd have a beer, too. But you can't get anything these days. Not to be had."

Sam's face looked vaguely hopeful as he eyed the noble. "We do need a gas engine bad, sir, for the tractor. Now that the central powercaster is gone, we got to have our own engines. I don't want to presume, sir, but—"

Donovan lifted one corner of his mouth in a tired smile. "I'm sorry," he said. "If I could get one machine for the whole community I'd be satisfied. Can't be done. We're trying to start a small factory of our own up at the manor, but it's slow work."

"I'm sure if anyone can do anything it's you, sir."

Donovan looked quizzically at the open countenance across the table. "Sam," he asked, "why do you people keep turning to the Family? We led you, and it was to defeat. Why do you want anything more to do with nobles? We're not even that, any longer. We've been stripped of our titles. We're just plain citizens of the Empire now like you, and the new rulers are Terran. Why do you still think of us as your leaders?"

"But you are, sir! You've always been. It wasn't the King's fault, or his men's, that Terra had so much more'n we did. We gave 'em a fight they won't forget in a hurry!"

"You were in my squadron, weren't you?"

"Yes, sir. CPO on the *Ansa Lancer*. I was with you at the Battle of Luga," The deep-set eyes glowed. "We hit, 'em there, didn't we, sir?"

"So we did." Donovan couldn't suppress the sudden fierce memory. Outnumbered, outgunned, half its ships shot to pieces and half the crews down with Sirius fever, the Royal Lansteaders had still made naval history and sent the Imperial Fleet kiyoodling back to Sol. Naval historians would be scratching their heads over that battle for the next five centuries. Before God, they'd fought!

HE BEGAN to sing the old war song, softly at first, louder as Sam joined him…

Comrades, hear the battle tiding,
hear the ships that rise and yell
faring outward, starward riding—
Kick the Terrans back to hell!

The others were listening, men raised weary heads, an old light burned in their eyes and tankards clashed together. They stood up to roar out the chorus till the walls shook.

Lift your glasses high,
kiss the girls goodbye,
(Live well, my friend, live well, live you well)
for we're riding, for we're riding,
for we're riding out to Terran sky! Terran
*   sky! Terran sky!*

We have shaken loose our thunder
where the planets have their way,
and the starry deeps of wonder
saw the Impies in dismay.
Lift your glasses high,
kiss the girls goodbye—

The workmen in the street heard it and stopped where they were. Some began to sing. The Imperial superintendent yelled, and an Ansan turned to flash him a wolfish grin. A squad of blue-uniformed Solarian marines coming toward the inn went on the double.

Oh, the Emp'ror sent his battle
ships against us in a mass,
but we shook them like a rattle
and we crammed them—

"Hi, there! Stop that!"

The song died, slowly and stubbornly, the men stood where they were and hands clenched into hard-knuckled fists. Someone shouted an obscenity.

The Terran sergeant was very young, and he felt unsure before those steady, hating eyes. He lifted his voice all the louder: "That will be enough of that. Any more and I'll run you all in for *lese majeste*. Haven't you drunken bums anything better to do than sit around swilling beer?"

A big Ansan smith laughed with calculated raucousness.

The sergeant looked around, trying to ignore him. "I'm here for Captain Donovan—Earl Basil, if you prefer. They said he'd be here. I've got an Imperial summons for him."

The noble stretched out a hand. "This is he. Let's have that paper."

"It's just the formal order," said the sergeant. "You're to come at once."

"Commoners," said Donovan quite mildly, "address me as 'sir.'"

"You're a commoner with the rest of 'em now." The sergeant's voice wavered just a little.

"I really must demand a little respect," said Donovan with drunken precision. There was an unholy gleam in his eyes.

"It's a mere formality, I know, but after all my family can trace itself farther back than the Empire, whereas you couldn't name your father."

Sam Olman snickered.

"Well, sir—" The sergeant tried elaborate sarcasm. "If you, sir, will please be so good as to pick your high-bred tail off that chair, sir, I'm sure the Imperium would be mostly deeply grateful to you, sir."

"I'll have to do without its gratitude, I'm afraid." Donovan folded the summons without looking at it and put it in his tunic pocket. "But thanks for the paper. I'll keep it in my bathroom."

"You're under arrest!"

Donovan stood slowly up, unfolding his sheer two meters of slender, wiry height. "All right, Wocha," he said. "Let's show them that Ansa hasn't surrendered yet."

He threw the tankard into the sergeant's face, followed it with the table against the two marines beside him, and vaulted over the sudden ruckus to drive a fist into the jaw of the man beyond.

Wocha rose and his booming cry trembled in the walls. He'd been a slave of Donovan's since he was a cub and the man a child, and if someone had liberated him he wouldn't have known what to do. As batman and irregular ground trooper he'd followed his master to the wars, and the prospect of new skull-breaking lit his eyes with glee.

For an instant there was tableau, Terrans and Ansans rigid, staring at the monster that suddenly stood behind the earl. The natives of Donarr have the not uncommon centauroid form, but their bodies are more like that of a rhinoceros than of a horse, hairless and slaty blue and enormously massive. The gorilla-armed torso ended in a round, muzzled, ape-like face, long-eared, heavy-jawed, with canine tusks hanging over the great gash of a mouth. A chair splintered under his feet, and he grinned.

"Paraguns—" cried the sergeant.

All hell let out for noon. Some of the customers huddled back into the corners but the rest smashed the ends off bottles and threw themselves against the Terrans. Sam Olman's remaining arm yanked a marine to him and bashed his face against the wall. Donovan's fist traveled a jolting arc to the nearest belly and he snatched a rifle loose and crunched it against the man's jaw. A marine seized him from behind. He twisted in the grip and kicked savagely, whirled around and drove the rifle butt into the larynx.

"Kill the blue-bellies! Kill the Impies! Hail, Ansa!"

Wocha charged into the squad, grabbed a hapless Terran in his four-fingered hands, and swung the man like a club. Someone drew his bayonet to stab the slave, it glanced off the thick skin and Wocha roared and sent him reeling. The riot blazed around the room, trampling men underfoot, shooting and cursing and swinging.

"Donovan, Donovan!" shouted Sam Olman. He charged the nearest Impy and got a bayonet in the stomach. He fell down, holding his hand to his wound, screaming.

The door was suddenly full of Terrans, marines arriving to help their comrades. Paraguns began to sizzle, men fell stunned before the supersonic beams and the fight broke up. Wocha charged the rescuers and a barrage sent his giant form crashing to the floor.

They herded the Ansans toward the city jail. Donovan, stirring on the ground as consciousness returned, felt handcuffs snap on his wrists.

IMPERIAL summons being what they were, he was bundled into a groundcar and taken under heavy guard toward the ordered place. He leaned wearily back, watching the streets blur past. Once a group of children threw stones at the vehicle.

"How about a cigarette?" he said.

"Shut up."

To his mild surprise, they did not halt at the military government headquarters—the old Hall of Justice where the Donovans had presided before the war—but went on toward the suburbs. The spaceport being still radioactive. They must be going to the emergency field outside the city. Hmm. He tried to relax. His head ached from the stun-beam.

A light cruiser had come in a couple of days before, H. M. *Ganymede*. It loomed enormous over the green rolling fields and the distance-blued hills and forests, a lance of bright metal and energy pointed into the clear sky of Ansa, blinding in the sun. A couple of spacemen on sentry at the gangway halted as the car stopped before them.

"This man is going to Commander Jansky."

"Aye, aye. Proceed."

Through the massive airlock, down the mirror-polished companionway, into an elevator and up toward the bridge— Donovan looked about him with a professional eye. The Impies kept a clean, tight ship, he had to admit.

He wondered if he would be shot, or merely imprisoned. He doubted if he'd committed an enslaving offense. Well, it had been fun, and there hadn't been a hell of a lot to live for anyway. Maybe his friends could spring him, if and when they got some kind of underground organized.

He was ushered into the captain's cabin. The ensign with him saluted. "Donovan as per orders, ma'm."

"Very good. But why is he in irons?"

"Resisted orders, ma'm. Started a riot. Bloody business."

"I—see." She nodded her dark head. "Losses?"

"I don't know, ma'm, but we had several wounded at least. A couple of Ansans were killed, I think."

"Well, leave him here. You may go."

"But—ma'm, he's dangerous!"

"I have a gun, and there's a man just outside the door. You may go, ensign."

Donovan swayed a little on his feet, trying to pull himself erect, wishing he weren't so dirty and bloody and generally messed up. You look like a tramp, man, he thought. Keep up appearances. Don't let them outdo us, even in spit and polish.

"Sit down, Captain Donovan," said the woman.

He lowered himself to a chair, raking her with deliberately insolent eyes. She was young to be wearing a commander's twin planets—young and trim and nice looking. Tall body, sturdy but graceful, well filled out in the blue uniform and red cloak; golden-blonde hair falling to her shoulders; strong blunt-fingered hands, one of them resting close to her sidearm. Her face was interesting, broad and cleanly molded, high cheekbones, wide full mouth, stubborn chin, snub nose, storm-gray eyes set far apart under heavy dark brows. A superior peasant type, he decided, and felt more at ease in the armor of his inbred haughtiness. He leaned back and crossed his legs.

"I am Helena Jansky, in command of this vessel," she said. Her voice was low and resonant, the note of strength in it. "I need you for a certain purpose. Why did you resist the Imperial summons?"

Donovan shrugged. "Let's say that I'm used to giving orders, not receiving them."

"Ah—yes." She ruffled the papers on her desk. "You were the Earl of Lanstead, weren't you?"

"After my father and older brother were killed in the war, yes." He lifted his head. "I am still the Earl."

She studied him with a dispassionate gaze that he found strangely uncomfortable. "I must say that you are a curious sort of leader," she murmured. "One who spends his time in a tavern getting drunk, and who on a whim provokes a disorder in which many of his innocent followers are hurt or killed, in which property difficult to replace is smashed—yes, I think it was about time that Ansa had a change of leadership."

Donovan's face was hot. Hell, take it, what right had she to tell him what to do? What right had the whole damned Empire to come barging in where it wasn't wanted? "The Families, under the King, have governed Ansa since it was colonized," he said stiffly. "If it had been such a misrule as you seem to think, would the commons have fought for us as they did?"

CHAPTER TWO

AGAIN that thoughtful stare. She saw a tall young man, badly disarrayed, blood and dirt streaking his long, thin-carved, curve-nosed features, an old scar jagging across his high narrow forehead. The hair was yellow, the eyes were blue, the whole look that of an old and settled aristocracy. His bitter voice lashed at her: "We ruled Ansa well because we were part of it, we grew up with the planet and we understood our folk and men were free under us. That's something that no upstart Solar Empire can have, not for centuries, not ever to judge by the stock they use for nobility. When peasants command spaceships—"

Her face grew a little pale, but she smiled and replied evenly, "I am the Lady Jansky of Torgandale on Valor—Sirius A IV—and you are now a commoner. Please remember that."

"All the papers in the Galaxy won't change the fact that your grandfather was a dirt farmer on Valor."

"He was an atomjack, and I'm proud of it. I suggest further that an aristocrat who has nothing to trade on but his pedigree is very ragged indeed. Now, enough of that." Her crisp tones snapped forth. "You've committed a serious offense, especially since this is still occupied territory. If you wish to cooperate with me, I can arrange for a pardon—also for your brawling friends. If not, the whole bunch of you can go to the mines."

Donovan shook his head, trying to clear it of alcohol and weariness and the ringing left by the parabeam. "Go on," he said, a little thickly. "I'll listen, anyway."

"What do you know of the Black Nebula?"

She must have seen his muscles jerk. For an instant he sat fighting himself, grasping at rigidity with all the strength that was in him, and the memory was a blaze and a shout and a stab of pure fear.

Valduma, Valduma!

The sudden thudding of his heart was loud in his ears, and he could feel the fine beads of sweat starting forth on his skin. He made a wrenching effort and pulled his mouth into a lopsided grin, but his voice wavered: "Which black nebula? There are a lot of them."

"Don't try to bait me." Her eyes were narrowed on him, and the fingers of one hand drummed the desktop. "You know I mean *the* Black Nebula. Nobody in this galactic sector speaks of any other."

"Why—well—" Donovan lowered his face to hide it till he could stiffen the mask, rubbing his temples with manacled hands. "It's just a nebula. A roughly spherical dust-cloud, maybe a light year in diameter, about ten parsecs from Ansa toward Sagittari. A few colonized stars on its fringes, nothing inside it as far as anyone knows. It has a bad name for some reason. The superstitious say it's haunted, and you hear stories of ships disappearing— Well, it gets a pretty wide berth. Not much out there anyway."

His mind was racing; he thought he could almost hear it *click* and *whirrr* as it spewed forth idea after idea, memory after memory. *Valduma and the blackness and they who laughed. The Nebula is pure poison, and now the Empire is getting interested. By heavens, it might poison them! Only would it stop there? This time they might decide to go on, to come out of the blackness.*

Jansky's voice seemed to come from very far away: "You know more than that, Donovan. Intelligence has been sifting Ansan records. You were the farthest-ranging space raider your planet had, and you had a base on Heim, at the very edge of the Nebula. Among your reports, there is an account of your men's unease, of the disappearance of small ships that cut through the Nebula on their missions, of ghostly things seen aboard other vessels and men who went mad. Your last report on the subject says that you investigated personally, that most of your crew went more or less crazy while in the Nebula, and that you barely got free. You recommend the abandonment of Heim and the suspension of operations in that territory. This was done, the region being of no great strategic importance anyway.

"Very well." The voice held a whip crack undertone. "What do you know about the Black Nebula?"

Donovan had fought his way back to impassivity. "You have about the whole story already," he said. "There were all sorts of illusions as we penetrated, whisperings and glimpses of impossible things and so on. It didn't affect me much, but it drove many toward insanity and some died. There was also very real and unexplainable trouble—engines, lights, and so on. My guess is that there's some sort of radiation in the Nebula that makes atoms and electrons misbehave; that'd affect the human nervous system too, of course. If you're thinking of entering it yourself, my only advice is—don't."

"Hmmm." She cupped her chin in her hand and looked down at the papers. "Frankly, we know very little about this galactic sector. Very few Terrans were ever here before the war, and previous intercourse on your part with Sol was even slighter. However, Intelligence has learned that the natives of almost every inhabited planet on the fringes of the Nebula worship it or at least regard it as the home of the gods."

"Well, it is a conspicuous object in their skies," said Donovan. He added truthfully enough: "I only know about Heim, where the native religion in the area of our base was a sort of devil-worship centered around the Nebula. They made big sacrifices—foodstuffs, furs, tools, and every conceivable item of use or luxury—which they claimed the devil-gods came and took. Some of the colonists thought there was something behind the legends, but I have my doubts." He shrugged. "Will that do?"

"For the time being." Jansky smiled with a certain bleak humor. "You can write a detailed report later on, and I strongly advise you not to mislead me. Because you're going there with us."

Donovan accepted the news coldly, but he thought the knocking of his heart must shake his whole body. His hands felt chilly and wet. "As you wish. Though what I can do—"

"You've been there before and know what to expect. Furthermore, you know the astrogation of that region; our charts are worse than sketchy, and even the Ansan tables have too many blank spots."

"Well—" Donovan got the words out slowly. "If I don't have to enlist. I will not take an oath to your Emperor."

"You needn't. Your status will be that of a civilian under Imperial command, directly responsible to me. You will have a cabin of your own, but no compensation except the abandonment of criminal proceedings against you." Jansky relaxed and her voice grew gentler. "However, if you serve well I'll see what I can do about pay. I daresay you could use some extra money."

"Thank you," said Donovan formally. He entered the first phase of the inchoate plan that was taking cloudy shape in his hammering brain. "May I have my personal slave with me? He's non-human, but he can eat Terran food."

Jansky smiled. There was sudden warmth in that smile, it made her human and beautiful. "As you wish if he doesn't have fleas. I'll write you an order for his embarkation."

She'd hit the ceiling when she found what kind of passenger she'd agreed to, thought Donovan. But by then it would be too late. *And, with Wocha to help me, and the ship blundering blind into the Nebula—Valduma, Valduma, I'm coming back! And this time will you kiss me or kill me?*

THE *Ganymede* lifted gravs and put the Ansa sun behind her. Much farther behind was Sol, an insignificant mote fifty light years away, lost in the thronging glory of stars. Ahead lay Sagittari, Galactic Center and the Black Nebula.

Space burned and blazed with a million bitter-bright suns, keen cold unwinking flames strewn across the utter dark of space, flashing and flashing over the hollow gulf of the leagues and the years. The Milky Way foamed in curdled silver around that enormous night, a shining girdle jeweled with the constellations. Far and far away wheeled the mysterious green and blue-white of the other galaxies, sparks of a guttering fire with a reeling immensity between. Looking toward the bows, one saw the great star clusters of Sagittari, the thronging host of suns burning and thundering at the heart of the Galaxy. *And what have we done?* thought Basil Donovan. *What is man and all his proud achievements? Our home star is a dwarf on the lonely fringe of the Galaxy, out where the stars thin away toward the great emptiness. We've ranged maybe two hundred light years from it in all directions and it's thirty thousand to the Center! Night and mystery and nameless immensities around us, our day of glory the briefest flicker on the edge of nowhere, then oblivion forever—and we won't be forgotten, because we'll never have been noticed. The Black Nebula is only the least and outermost of the great clouds that thicken toward the Center and hide its ultimate heart from us, it is nothing even as we, and yet it holds a power older than the human race and a terror that may whelm it.*

He felt again the old quailing funk; fear crawled along his spine and will drained out of his soul. He wanted to run, escape, huddle under the sky of Ansa to hide from the naked blaze of the universe, live out his day and forget that he had seen the scornful face of God. But there was no turning back, not now, the ship was already outpacing light on her secondary drive and he was half a prisoner aboard. He squared his shoulders and walked away from the view-plate, back toward his cabin.

Wocha was sprawled on a heap of blankets, covering the floor with his bulk. He was turning the brightly colored pages of a child's picture book. "Boss," he asked, "when do we kill 'em?"

"The Impies? Not yet, Wocha. Maybe not at all." Donovan stepped over the monster and lay down on his bunk, hands behind his head. He could feel the thrum of the driving engines, quivering in the ship and his bones. "The Nebula may do that for us."

"We go back there?" Wocha stirred uneasily. "I don't like, boss. It's toombar. Bad."

"Yeah, so it is."

"Better we stay home. Manor needs repair. Peasants need our help. I need beer."

"So do I. I'll see if we can't promote some from the quartermaster. Old John can look after the estate while we're away, and the peasants will just have to look after themselves. Maybe it's time they learned how." At a knock on the door: "Come in."

Tetsuo Takahashi, the ship's exec, brought his small sturdy form around Wocha and sat down on the edge of the bunk. "Your slave has the Old Lady hopping mad," he grinned. "He'll eat six times a man's ration."

"And drink it." Donovan smiled back; he couldn't help liking the cocky little Terran. Then, with a sudden renewed bitterness: "And he's worth it. I couldn't be without him. He may not be so terribly bright, but he's my only proof that loyalty and decency aren't extinct."

Takahashi gave him a puzzled look. "Why do you hate us so much?" he asked.

"You came in where you weren't asked. Ansa was free, and now it's just another province of your damned Empire."

"Maybe so. But you were a backwater, an under-populated agricultural planet that nobody had ever heard of, exposed to barbarian raids and perhaps to nonhuman conquest. You're safe now, and you're part of a great social-economic system that can do more than all those squabbling little kingdoms and republics and theocracies and lord knows what else put together could ever dream of."

"Who said we wanted to be safe? Our ancestors came to Ansa to be free. We fought Shalmu when the greenies wanted to take what we'd built, and then we made friends with them. We had elbowroom and a way of life that was our own. Now you'll bring in your surplus population to fill our green lands with yelling cities and squalling people. You'll tear down the culture we evolved so painfully and make us just another bunch of kowtowing Imperial citizens."

"Frankly, Donovan, I don't think it was much of a culture. It sat in its comfortable rut and admired the achievements of its ancestors. What did your precious Families do but hunt and loaf and throw big parties? Maybe they did fulfill a magisterial function—so what? Any elected fool could do the same in that simple a society." Takahashi fixed his eyes on Donovan's. "But rights and wrongs aside, the Empire had to annex Ansa, and when you wouldn't come in peaceably you had to be dragged in."

"Yeah. A dumping ground for people who were too stupid not to control their own breeding."

"Your Ansan peasants, my friend, have about twice the Terran birth rate. It's merely that there are more Terrans to start with—and Sirians and Centaurians and all the old settled planets. No, it was more than that. It was a question of military necessity."

"Uh-huh. Sure."

"Read your history sometime. When the Commonwealth broke up in civil wars two hundred years ago it was hell between the stars. Half-savage peoples who never should have left their planets had learned how to build spaceships and were going out to raid and conquer. A dozen would-be overlords scorched whole worlds with their battles. You can't have anarchy on an interstellar scale. Too many people suffer. Old Manuel the First had the guts to proclaim himself Emperor of Sol—no pretty euphemisms for him, an empire was needed and an empire was what he built. He kicked the barbarians out of the Solar System and went on to conquer their home territories and civilize them. That meant he had to subjugate stars closer to home, to protect his lines of communication. This led to further trouble elsewhere. Oh, yes, a lot of it was greed, but the planets that were conquered for their wealth would have been sucked in anyway by sheer economics. The second Argolid carried on, and now his son, Manuel II, is finishing the job. We've very nearly attained what we must have—an empire large enough to be socio-economically self-sufficient and defend itself against all comers, of which there are many, without being too large for control. You should visit the inner Empire sometime, Donovan, and see how many social evils it's been possible to wipe out because of security and central power. But we need this sector to protect our Sagittarian flank, so we're taking it. Fifty years from now you'll be glad we did."

DONOVAN looked sourly up at him. "Why in the devil are you feeding me all that?" he asked. "I've heard it all before."

"We're going to survey a dangerous region, and you're our guide. The captain and I think there's more than a new radiation in the Black Nebula. I'd like to think we could trust you."

"Think so if you wish."

"We could use a hypnoprobe on you, you know. We'd squeeze your skull dry of everything it contained. But we'd rather spare you that indignity."

"And you might need me when you get there, and I'd still be only half conscious. Quit playing the great altruist, Takahashi."

The exec shook his head. "There's something wrong inside you, Donovan," he murmured. "You aren't the man who licked us at Luga."

"Luga!" Donovan's eyes flashed. "Were you there?"

"Sure. Destroyer *North Africa*, just come back from the Zarune front— Cigarette?"

They fell to yarn-filled conversation and passed a pleasant hour. Donovan could not suppress a vague regret when Takahashi left. *They aren't such bad fellows, those Impies. They were brave and honorable enemies, and they've been lenient conquerors as such things go. But when we hit the Black Nebula—*

He shuddered. "Wocha, get that whiskey out of my trunk."

"You not going to get drunk again, boss?" The Donarrian's voice rumbled disappointment.

"I am. And I'm going to try to stay drunk the whole damn voyage. You just don't know what we're heading for, Wocha."

Stranger, go back.
Spaceman, go home. Turn back, adventurer.
It is death. Return, human.

The darkness whispered. Voices ran down the length of the ship, blending with the unending murmur of the drive, urging, commanding, whispering so low that it seemed to be within men's skulls.

Basil Donovan lay in darkness. His mouth tasted foul, and there was a throb in his temples and a wretchedness in his throat. He lay and listened to the voice, which had wakened him.

Go home, wanderer. You will die, your ship will plunge through the hollow dark till the stars grow cold. Turn home, human.

"Boss. I hear them, boss. I'm scared."

"How long have we been underway? When did we leave Ansa?"

"A week ago, boss, maybe more. You been drunk. Wake up, boss, turn on the light. They're whispering in the dark, and I'm scared."

"We must be getting close."

Return. Go home. First comes madness and then comes death and then comes the spinning outward forever. Turn back, spaceman.

Bodiless whisper out of the thick thrumming dark, sourceless all-pervading susurration, and it mocked, there was the cruel cynical scorn of the outer vastness running up and down the laughing voice. It murmured, it jeered, it ran along nerves with little icy feet and flowed through the brain, it called and gibed and hungered. It wanted them to go back, and it knew they wouldn't and railed its mockery at them for it. Demon whisper, there in the huge cold loneliness, sneering and grinning and waiting.

Donovan sat up and groped for the light switch. "We're close enough," he said tonelessly. "We're in their range now."

Footsteps racketed in the corridor outside. A sharp rap on his door. "Come in. Come in and enjoy yourself."

CHAPTER THREE

DONOVAN hadn't found the switch before the door was open and light spilled in from the hallway fluorotubes. Cold white light, a shaft of it picking out Wocha's monstrous form an throwing grotesque shadows on the walls. Commander Jansky was there, in full uniform, and Ensign Jeanne Scoresby, her aide. The younger girl's face was white, her eyes enormous, but Jansky wore grimness like an armor.

"All right, Donovan," she said. "You've had your binge, and now the trouble is starting. You didn't say they were voices."

"They could be anything," he answered, climbing out of the bunk and steadying himself with one hand. His head swam a little. The corners of the room were thick with shadow.

Back, spaceman. Turn home, human.

"Delusions?" The man laughed unpleasantly. His face was pale and gaunt, unshaven in the bleak radiance. "When you start going crazy, I imagine you always hear voices."

There was contempt in the gray eyes that raked him. "Donovan, I put a technician to work on it when the noises began a few hours ago. He recorded them. They're very faint, and they seem to originate just outside the ear of anyone who hears them, but they're real enough. Radiations don't speak in human Anglic with an accent such as I never heard before. Not unless they're carrier waves for a message. Donovan, who or what is inside the Black Nebula?"

The Ansan's laugh jarred out again. "Who or what is inside this ship?" he challenged. "Our great human science has no way of making the air vibrate by itself. Maybe there are ghosts, standing invisible just beside us and whispering in our ears."

"We could detect nothing, no radiations, no energy-fields, nothing but the sounds themselves. I refuse to believe that matter can be set in motion without some kind of physical force being applied." Jansky clapped a hand to her sidearm. "*You* know what is waiting for us. *You* know how they do it."

"Go ahead. Hypnoprobe me. Lay me out helpless for a week. Or shoot me if you like. You'll be just as dead whatever you do."

Her tones were cold and sharp. "Get on your clothes and come up to the bridge."

He shrugged, picked up his uniform, and began to shuck his pajamas. The women looked away.

Human, go back. You will go mad and die.

Valduma; he thought, with a wrenching deep inside him. *Valduma, I've returned.*

He stepped over to the mirror. The Ansan uniform was a gesture of defiance, and it occurred to him that he should shave if he wore it in front of these Terrans. He ran the electric razor over cheeks and chin, pulled his tunic straight, and turned back. "All right."

They went out into the hallway. A spaceman went by on some errand. His eyes were strained wide, staring at blankness, and his lips moved. The voices were speaking to him.

"It's demoralizing the crew," said Jansky. "It has to stop."

"Go ahead and stop it," jeered Donovan. "Aren't you the representative of the almighty Empire of Sol? Command them in the name of His Majesty to stop."

"The crew, I mean," she said impatiently. "They've got no business being frightened by a local phenomenon."

"Any human would be," answered Donovan. "You are, too, though you won't admit it. I am. We can't help ourselves. It's instinct."

"Instinct?" Her clear eyes were a little surprised.

"Sure." Donovan halted before a viewscreen. Space blazed and roiled against the reaching darkness. "Just look out there. It's the primeval night, it's the blind unknown where unimaginable inhuman Powers are abroad. We're still the old half-ape, crouched over his fire and trembling while the night roars around us. Our lighted, heated, metal-armored ship is still the lonely cave-fire, the hearth with steel and stone laid at the door to keep out the gods. When the Wild Hunt breaks through and shouts at us, we must be frightened, it's the primitive fear of the dark. It's part of us."

She swept on, her cloak a scarlet wing flapping behind her. They took the elevator to the bridge.

Donovan had not watched the Black Nebula grow over the days; he did not see it swell to a monstrous thing that blotted out half the sky, lightlessness fringed with the cold glory of the stars. Now that the ship was entering its tenuous outer fringes, the heavens on either side were blurring and dimming, and the blackness yawned before. Even the densest nebula is a hard vacuum; but tons upon incredible tons of cosmic dust and gas, reaching planetary and interstellar distances on every hand, will blot out the sky. It was like rushing into an endless, bottomless hole; the ship was falling and falling into the pit of Hell.

"I noticed you never looked bow-wards on the trip," said Jansky. There was steel in her voice. "Why did you lock yourself in your cabin and drink like a sponge?"

"I was bored," he replied sullenly.

"You were afraid!" she snapped contemptuously. "You didn't dare watch the Nebula growing. Something happened the last time you were here that sucked the guts out of you."

"Didn't your Intelligence talk to the men who were with me?"

"Yes, of course. None of them would say more than you've said. They all wanted us to come here, but blind and unprepared. Well, Mister Donovan, we're going in!"

The floor-plates shook under Wocha's tread. "You not talk to boss that way," he rumbled.

"Let be, Wocha," said Donovan. "It doesn't matter how she talks."

He looked ahead, and the old yearning came alive in him, the fear and the memory, but he had not thought that it would shiver with such a strange gladness.

And—who knew? A bargain—

Valduma, come back to me!

Jansky's gaze on him narrowed, but her voice was suddenly low and puzzled. "You're smiling," she whispered. He turned from the viewscreen and his laugh was ragged. "Maybe I'm looking forward to this visit, Helena."

"My name," she said stiffly, "is Commander Jansky."

"Out there, maybe. But in here there is no rank, no Empire, no mission. We're all humans, frightened little humans huddling together against the dark." Donovan's smile softened. "You know, Helena, you have very beautiful eyes."

The slow flush crept up her high smooth cheeks. "I want a full report of what happened to you last time," she said. "Now. Or you go under the probe."

Wanderer, it is a long way home. Spaceman, spaceman, your sun is very far away.

"Why, certainly." Donovan leaned against the wall and grinned at her. "Glad to. Only you won't believe me."

28

She made no reply, but folded her arms and waited. The ship trembled with its forward thrust. Sweat beaded the forehead of the watch officer and he glared around him.

"We're entering the home of all lawlessness," said Donovan. "The realm of magic, the outlaw world of werebeasts and nightgangers. Can't you hear the wings outside? These ghosts are only the first sign. We'll have a plague of witches soon."

"Get out!" she said.

He shrugged. "All right, Helena. I told you you wouldn't believe me." He turned and walked slowly from the bridge.

OUTSIDE was starless, lightless, infinite black. The ship crept forward, straining her detectors, groping into the blind dark while her crew went mad.

Spaceman, it is too late. You will never find your way home again. You are dead men on a ghost ship, and you will fall forever into the Night.

"I saw him, Wong, I saw him down in Section Three, tall and thin and black. He laughed at me, and then there wasn't anything there."

Sound of great wings beating somewhere outside the hull.

Mother, can I have him? Can I have his skull to play with?

Not yet, child. Soon. Soon.

Wicked rain of laughter and the sound of clawed feet running.

No one went alone. Spacemen First Class Gottfried and Martinez went down a starboard companionway and saw the hooded black form waiting for them. Gottfried pulled out his blaster and fired. The ravening beam sprang backward and consumed him. Martinez lay mumbling in psychobay.

The lights went out. After an hour they flickered back on again, but men had rioted and killed each other in the dark.

Commander Jansky recalled all personal weapons on the grounds that the crew could no longer be trusted with them. The men drew up a petition to get them back. When it was refused, there was muttering of revolt.

Spacemen, you have wandered too far. You have wandered beyond the edge of creation, and now there is only death.

The hours dragged into days. When the ship's timepieces started disagreeing, time ceased to have meaning.

Basil Donovan sat in his cabin. There was a bottle in his hand, but he tried to go slow. He was waiting.

When the knock came, he leaped from his seat and every nerve tightened up and screamed. He swore at himself. They wouldn't knock when they came for him. "Go on, enter—" His voice wavered.

Helena Jansky stepped inside, closing the door after her. She had thinned, and there was darkness in her eyes, but she still bore herself erect. Donovan had to salute the stubborn courage that was in her. The unimaginative peasant blood— no, it was more than that, she was as intelligent as he, but there was a deep strength in that tall form, a quiet vitality that had perhaps been bred out of the Families of Ansa. "Sit down," he invited.

She sighed and ran a hand through her golden hair. "Thanks."

"Drink?"

"No. Not on duty."

"And the captain is always on duty. Well, let it go." Donovan lowered himself to the bunk beside her, resting his feet on Wocha's columnar leg. The Donarrian muttered and whimpered in his sleep.

"What can I do for you?" Donovan asked.

Her gaze was steady and grave. "You can tell me the truth."

"About the Nebula? Why should I? Give me one good reason why an Ansan should care what happens to a Solarian ship."

"Perhaps only that we're all human beings here, that those boys have earth and rain and sunlight and wives waiting for them."

And Valduma—no, she isn't human. Fire and ice and storming madness, but not human. Too beautiful to be flesh.

"This trip was your idea," he said defensively.

"Donovan, you wouldn't have played such a foul trick and made such a weak, self-righteous excuse in the old days."

He looked away, feeling his cheeks hot.

"Well," he mumbled, "why not turn around, get out of the Nebula if you can, and maybe come back later with a task force?"

"And lead them all into this trap? Our subtronics are out, you know. We can't send information back, so we'll just go on and learn a little more and then try to fight our way home."

His smile was crooked. "I may have been baiting you, Helena. But if I told you everything I know, it wouldn't help. There isn't enough."

Her hand fell strong and urgent on his. "Tell me, then! Tell me anyway."

"But there is so little. There's a planet somewhere in the Nebula, and it has inhabitants with powers I don't begin to understand. But among other things, they can project themselves hyperwise, just like a spaceship, without needing engines to do it. And they have a certain control over matter and energy."

"The fringe stars—these beings in the Nebula really have been their 'gods'?"

"Yes. They've projected themselves, terrorized the natives for centuries, and carry home the sacrificial materials for their own use. They're doubtless responsible for all the ships around here that never came home. They don't like visitors." Donovan saw her smile, and his own lips twitched. "But they did, I suppose, take some prisoners, to learn our language and anything else they could about us."

She nodded. "I'd conjectured as much. If you don't accept theories involving the supernatural, and I don't, it follows almost necessarily. If a few of them projected themselves aboard and hid somewhere, they could manipulate air molecules from a distance so as to produce the whisperings—" She smiled afresh, but the hollowness was still in her.

"When you call it a new sort of ventriloquism, it doesn't sound nearly so bad, does it?"

Fiercely, the woman turned on him. "And what have you had to do with them? How are you so sure?"

"I—talked with one of them," he replied slowly. "You might say we struck up a friendship of sorts. But I learned nothing, and the only benefit I got was escaping. I've no useful information." His voice sharpened. "And that's all I have to say."

"Well, we're going on!" Her head lifted pridefully.

Donovan's smile was a crooked grimace. He took her hand, and it lay unresisting between his fingers. "Helena," he said, "you've been trying to psychoanalyze me this whole trip. Maybe it's my turn now. You're not so hard as you tell yourself."

"I am an officer of the Imperial Navy." Her haughtiness didn't quite come off.

"Sure, sure. A hard-shelled career girl. Only you're also a healthy human being. Down underneath, you want a home and kids and quiet green hills. Don't lie to yourself. That wouldn't be fitting to the Lady Jansky of Torgandale, would it? You went into service because it was the thing to do.

And you're just a scared kid, my dear." Donovan shook his head. "But a very nice-looking kid."

Tears glimmered on her lashes. "Stop it," she whispered desperately. "Don't say it."

He kissed her, a long slow kiss with her mouth trembling under his and her body shivering ever so faintly. The second time she responded, shy as a child, hardly aware of the sudden hunger.

SHE pulled free then, sat with eyes wide and wild, one hand lifted to her mouth. "No," she said, so quietly he could scarcely hear. "No, not now—"

Suddenly she got up and almost fled. Donovan sighed.

Why did I do that? To stop her inquiring too closely? Or just because she's honest and human, and Valduma isn't? Or—

Darkness swirled before his eyes. Wocha came awake and shrank against the farther wall, terror rattling in his throat. "Boss—boss, she's here again—"

Donovan sat unstirring, elbows on knees, bands hanging empty, and looked at the two who had come. "Hello, Valduma," he said.

"Basil—" Her voice sang against him, rippling, lilting, the unending sharp laughter beneath its surprise. "Basil, you have come back."

"Uh-huh." He nodded at the other. "You're Morzach, aren't you? Sit down. Have a drink. Old home week."

The creature from Arzun remained erect.

He looked human on the outside, tall and gaunt in a black cape, which glistened with tiny points of starlight, the hood thrown back so that his red hair fell free to his shoulders. The face was long and thin, chiseled to an ultimate refinement of classical beauty, white and cold. Cold as space-tempered steel, in spite of the smile on the pale lips, in spite of the dark mirth in the slant green eyes. One hand rested on the jeweled hilt of a sword.

Valduma stood beside Morzach for an instant, and Donovan watched her with the old sick wildness rising and clamoring in him.

You are the fairest thing that was ever between the stars, you are ice and flame and living fury, stronger and weaker than man, cruel and sweet as a child a thousand years old, and I love you. But you are not human, Valduma.

She was tall, and her grace was a lithe rippling flow, wind and fire and music made flesh, a burning glory of hair rushing past her black-caped shoulders, hands slim and beautiful, the strange clean-molded face white as polished ivory, the mouth red and laughing, the eyes long and oblique and gold-flecked green. When she spoke, it was like singing in Heaven and laughter in Hell. Donovan looked at her, not moving.

"Basil, you came back to me?"

"He came because he had to." Morzach of Arzun folded his arms, eyes smoldering in anger. "Best we kill him now."

"Later, perhaps later, but not now," Valduma laughed aloud.

Suddenly she was in Donovan's arms. Her kisses were a rain of fire. There was thunder and darkness and dancing stars. He was aware of nothing else, not for a long, long time.

She leaned back in his grasp, smiling up at him, stroking his hair with one slender hand.

His cheek was bloody where she had scratched him. He looked back into her eyes—they were cat's eyes, split-pupiled, all gold and emerald without the human white. She laughed very softly. "Shall I kill you now?" she whispered. "Or drive you mad first? Or let you go again? What would be most amusing, Basil?"

"This is no time for your pranks," said Morzach sharply. "We have to deal with this ship. It's getting dangerously close to Arzun, and we've been unable yet to break the morale and discipline of the crew. I think the only way is to wreck the ship."

"Wreck it on Arzun, yes!" Valduma's laughter pulsed and throbbed. "Bring them to their goal. Help them along, even. Oh, yes, Morzach, it is a good thought."

"We'll need your help," said the creature-man to Donovan. "'I take it that you're guiding them. You must encourage them to offer no resistance when we take over the controls. Our powers won't stand too long against atomic energy."

"Why should I help you?" Donovan's tone was hoarse. "What can you give me?

"If you live," said Valduma, "and can make your way to Drogobych, I might give you much." She laughed again, maniacal laughter that did not lose its music. "That would be diverting!"

"I don't know," he groaned. "'I don't know—I thought a bargain could be made, but now I wonder."

"I leave him to you," said Morzach sardonically, and vanished.

"Basil," whispered Valduma, "Basil, I have—sometimes—missed you."

"Get out, Wocha," said Donovan.

"Boss—she's toombar—"

"Get out!"

Wocha lumbered slowly from the cabin. There were tears in his eyes.

CHAPTER FOUR

THE *Ganymede's* engines rose to full power and the pilot controls spun over without a hand on them.

"Engine room! Engine room! Stop that nonsense down there!"

"We can't—they're frozen—the converter has gone into full without us——"

"Sir, I can't budge this stick. It's locked somehow.

The lights went out. Men screamed.

"Get me a flashlight!" snapped Takahashi in the dark. "I'll take this damned panel apart myself."

The beam etched his features against night. "Who goes?" he cried.

"It's I." Jansky appeared in the dim reflected glow. "Never mind, Takahashi. Let the ship have her way."

"But ma'm, we could crash——"

"I've finally gotten Donovan to talk. He says we're in the grip of some kind of power-beam. They'll pull us to one of their space stations and then maybe we can negotiate—or fight. Come on, we've got to quiet the men.

The flashlight went out. Takahashi's laugh was shrill. "Better quiet me first, Captain."

Her hand was on his arm, steadying, strengthening. "Don't fail me, Tetsuo. You're the last one I've got. I just had to paralyze Scoresby."

"Thanks—thanks, chief. I'm all right now. Let's go."

They fumbled through blindness. The engines roared, full speed ahead with a ghost on the bridge. Men were stumbling and cursing and screaming in the dark. Someone switched on the battle-stations siren, and its howl was the last voice of insanity.

Struggle in the dark, wrestling, paralyzing the berserk, calling on all the iron will that had lifted humankind to the stars—slow restoration of order, men creeping to general quarters, breathing heavily in the guttering light of paper torches.

The engines cut off and the ship snapped into normal matter state. Helena Jansky saw blood-red sunlight through the viewport. There was no time to sound the alarm before the ship crashed.

"A HUNDRED men. No more than a hundred men alive."

She wrapped her cloak tight about her against the wind and stood looking across the camp. The streaming firelight touched her face with red, limning it against the utter dark of the night heavens, sheening faintly in the hair that blew wildly around her strong bitter countenance. Beyond, other fires danced and flickered in the gloom; men huddled around them while the cold seeped slowly to their bones. Here and there an injured human moaned.

Across the ragged spine of bare black hills they could still see the molten glow of the wreck. When it hit, the atomic converters had run wild and begun devouring the hull. There had barely been time for the survivors to drag themselves and some of the cripples free, and to put the rocky barrier between them and the mounting radioactivity. During the slow red sunset, they had gathered wood, hewing with knives at the distorted scrub trees reaching above the shale and snow of the valley.

Now they sat waiting out the night.

Takahashi shuddered. "It's so cold!"

"It'll get colder," said Donovan tonelessly. "This is an old planet of an old red dwarf sun. Its rotation has slowed. The nights are long."

"How do you know?" Lieutenant Elijah Cohen glued at him out of a crudely bandaged face. The firelight made his eyes gleam red. "How do you know unless you're in with them? Unless you arranged this yourself?"

Wocha reached forth a massive fist. "You shut up," he rumbled.

"Never mind," said Donovan. "I just thought some things would be obvious. You saw the star, so you should know it's the type of a burned-out dwarf. Since planets are formed at an early stage of a star's evolution, this world must be old too. Look at these rocks—citrified, back when the stellar energy output got really high just before the final collapse; and nevertheless eroded down to hare snags. That takes millions of years."

He reflected that his reasoning, while sound enough, was based on foreknown conclusions. *Cohen's right. I have betrayed them. It was Valduma, watching over me, who brought Wocha and myself unhurt through the crash. I saw, Valduma, I saw you with your hair flying in the chaos, riding witch-like through sundering ruin, and you were laughing. Laughing!* He felt ill.

"Nevertheless, the planet has a thin but breathable atmosphere, frozen water, and vegetable life," said Takahashi. "Such things don't survive the final rot stage of a sun without artificial help. This planet has natives. Since we were deliberately crashed here, I daresay the natives are our earlier friends." He turned dark accusing eyes on the Ansan. "How about it, Donovan?"

"I suppose you're right," he answered. "I knew there was a planet in the Nebula, the natives had told me that in my previous trip. This star lies near the Center, in a 'hollow' region where there isn't enough dust to force the planet into its primary, and shares a common velocity with the Nebula. It stays here, in other words."

"You told me—" Helena Jansky bit her lip, then slowly forced the words out. "You told me, and I believed you, that there was nothing immediately to fear when the Nebulites took over our controls. So we didn't fight them; we didn't try to overcome their forces with our own engines. And it cost us the ship and over half the crew."

"I told you what happened to me last time," he lied steadfastly. "I can't help it if things were different this trip."

She turned her back. The wind blew a thin hissing veil of dry snow across her ankles. A wounded man suddenly screamed out there in the dark.

How does it feel, Donovan? You made her trust you and then betrayed her for a thing that isn't even human. How does it feel to be a Judas?

"NEVER mind recriminations," said Takahashi. "This isn't the time to hold trials. We've got to decide what to do."

"They have a city on this planet," said Donovan. "Drogobych, they call it, and the planet's name is Arzun. It lies somewhere near the equator, they told me once. If they meant us to make our own way to it—and it would be like them—then it may well lie due south. We can march that way, assuming that the sun set in the west."

"Nothing to lose," shrugged the Terran.

"But we haven't many weapons, a few assorted sidearms is all, and they aren't much use against these creatures anyway."

Something howled out in the darkness. The ground quivered, ever so faintly, to the pounding of heavy feet.

"Wild animals yet!" Cohen grinned humorlessly. "Better sound battle stations, Captain."

"Yes, yes, I suppose so." She blew her whistle, a thin shrilling in the windy dark. As she turned around, Donovan saw a gleam running along her cheek. Tears?

The noise came closer. They heard the rattle of claws on stone. The Terrans moved together, guns in front, clubs and rocks and bare hands behind. They have guts, thought Donovan. Oh do they have guts!

"Food would be scarce on a barren planet like this," said Ensign Chundra Dass. "We seem to be elected."

The hollow roar sounded, echoing between the hills and caught up by the thin harrying wind. "Hold fire," said Helena. Her voice was clear and steady. "Don't waste charges. Wait—"

The thing leaped out of darkness, a ten-meter length of gaunt scaled body and steel-hard claws and whipping tail, soaring through the snow-streaked air and caught in the vague uneasy firelight. Helena's blaster crashed, a lightning bolt sizzled against the armored head.

The monster screamed. Its body tumbled shatteringly among the humans, it seized a man in its jaws and shook him and trampled another underfoot. Takahashi stepped forward and shot again at its dripping wound. The blaster bolt zigzagged wildly off the muzzle of his gun.

Even the animals can do it—!

"I'll get him, boss!" Wocha reared on his hind legs, came down again with a thud, and charged. Stones flew from beneath his feet. The monster's tail swept out; a man tumbled before it with his ribs caved in, and Wocha staggered as he caught the blow. Still he rushed in, clutching the barbed end of the tail to his breast. The monster writhed, bellowing. Another blaster bolt hit it from the rear. It turned and a shot at its eyes veered away.

Wocha hit it with all the furious momentum he had. He rammed its spear-like tail down the open jaws and blood spurted. "Ho, Donovan!" he shouted. As the thing screamed and snapped at him, he caught its jaws in his hands.

"Wocha!" yelled Donovan. "Wocha!" He ran wildly toward the fight.

The Donarrian's great back arched with strain. It was as if they could hear his muscles crack. Slowly, slowly, he forced the jaws wider. The monster lashed its body, pulling him to his knees, dragging him over the ground, and still he fought.

"Damn you," he roared in the whirling dust and snow, "hold still!"

The jaws broke. And the monster screamed once more, and then it wasn't there. Wocha tumbled over.

Donovan fell across him, sobbing, laughing, cursing. Wocha picked him up. "You all right, boss?" he asked. "You well?"

"Yes—yes—oh, you blind bloody fool! You stupid, blundering ass!" Donovan hugged him.

"Gone," said Helena. "It vanished."

They picked up their dead and wounded and returned to the fires. The cold bit deep. Something else hooted out in the night.

It was a long time before Takahashi spoke. "You might expect it," he said. "These parapsychical powers don't come from nowhere. The intelligent race, our enemies of Drogobych, simply have them highly developed; the animals do to a lesser extent. I think it's a matter of life being linked to the primary atomic probabilities, the psi functions that give the continuous-field distribution of matter-energy in space-time. In a word, control of external matter and energy by conscious will acting through the unified field that is space-time. Telekinesis."

"Uh-huh," said Dass wearily. "Even some humans have a slight para-power. Control dice or electron beams or what have you. But why aren't the—what did you call them? — Arzunians overrunning the Galaxy?"

"They can only operate over a certain range, which happens to be about the distance to the fringe stars," said Donovan. "Beyond that distance, dispersion limits them, plus the fact that differences of potential energy must be made up from their own metabolism. The animals, of course, have very limited range, a few kilometers perhaps. The Arzunians use telekinesis to control matter and energy, and the same subspatial principles as our ships to go faster than light. Only since they aren't lugging around a lot of hull and passengers and assorted machinery—just themselves and a little air and maybe an armful of sacrificial goods from a fringe planet. They don't need atomic engines.

"They aren't interested in conquering the Galaxy. Why should they be? They can get all their needs and luxuries from the peoples to whom they are gods. An old race, very old, decadent if you will. But they don't like interference."

Takahashi looked at him sharply. "I glimpsed one of them on the ship," he said. "He carried a spear."

"Yeah. Another reason why they aren't conquerors. They have no sense for mechanics at all. Never had any reason to evolve one when they could manipulate matter directly without more than the simplest tools. They're probably more intelligent than humans in an all-around way, but they don't have the type of brain and the concentration needed to learn physics and chemistry. Aren't interested, either."

"So, swords against guns... We may have a chance!"

"They can turn your missiles, remember. Guns are little use, you have to distract them or they don't notice your shot till too late. But they can't control you. They aren't telepaths and their type of matter-control is heterodyned by living nerve currents. You could kill one of them with a sword where a gun would most likely kill you."

SARGASSO OF LOST STARSHIPS

"I—see—" Helena looked strangely at him. "You're becoming very vocal all of a sudden."

Donovan rubbed his eyes and shivered in the cold. "What of it? Yon wanted the truth. You're getting it."

Why am I telling them? Why am I not just leading them to the slaughter as Valduma wanted? Is it that I can't stand the thought of Helena being hunted like a beast?

Whose side am I on? he thought wildly. Takahashi gestured and his voice came eager. "That's it. That's it! The ship scattered assorted metal and plastic over twenty hectares as she fell. Safe for us to gather up tomorrow. We can use our blaster flames to shape weapons. Swords, axes, spears. By the Galaxy, we'll arm ourselves and then we'll march on Drogobych!"

CHAPTER FIVE

IT WAS a strange little army, thought Donovan, as strange as any the Galaxy had ever seen.

He looked back. The old ruined highway went down a narrow valley between sheer cliffs of eroded black stone reaching up toward the deep purplish heaven. The sun was wheeling westerly, a dull red ember throwing light like dotted blood on the dreariness of rock and ice and gaunt gray trees; a few snowflakes, borne on a thin chill wind, drifted across the path of march. A lonely bird, cruel-beaked and watchful, hovered on great black wings far overhead, waiting for them to die.

The men of the Imperial Solar Navy walked close together. They were haggard and dirty and bearded, clad in such ragged articles as they had been able to salvage, armed with the crudely forged weapons of a vanished age, carrying their sick and wounded on rude litters. Ghost world, ghost army, marching through an echoing windy solitude to its unknown weird—but men's faces were still brave, and one of them was singing. The sunburst banner of the Empire flapped above then, the one splash of color in the great murky landscape.

Luck had been with them, of a sort. Game animals had appeared in more abundance than one would have thought the region could support, deer-like things, which they shot for meat to supplement their iron rations. They had stumbled on the old highway and followed its arrow-straight course southward. Many days and many tumbled hollow ruins of great cities lay behind them, and still they trudged on.

Luck? wondered Donovan. *I think it was intentional. I think the Arzunians want us to reach Drogobych.*

He heard the scrape of boots on the slanting hillside behind him, and turned around to face Helena. He stopped and smiled. There bad been a slow unspoken intimacy growing between them as they worked and struggled together. Not many words, but the eyes of each would often stray to the other, and a hand would brush over a hand as if by accident. Tired and hungry and road-stained, cap set askew on tangled hair, skin reddened by wind and blued with cold, she was still good to look on.

"Why are you walking so far from the road?" she asked.

"Oh, serving as outrider, maybe," he said, resuming his stride. She fell into step beside him. "Up here you get a wider view."

"Do you think we have much further to go, Basil?"

He shrugged.

"We'd never have come this far without you," she said, looking down at her scuffed boots. "You and Wocha and Takahashi."

"Maybe the Empire will send a rescue mission when we don't come back," he suggested.

"No doubt they will. But they can't find one little star in this immensity. Even thermocouples won't help; the Nebula diffuses radiation too much. And they'd be blundering into the same trap as we." Helena looked up. "No, Basil, we've got to fight our way clear alone."

There was a long stretch of thicket growing on the hillside. Donovan went along the right of it, cutting off view of the army. "You know," he said, "you and those boys down there make me feel a lot kinder toward the Empire."

"Thank you. Thank you. We—" She took his arm. "It's a question of unifying the human race, ultimately this whole region of stars, and—*Oh!*"

The beasts were suddenly there in front of them, lean black things, which snarled with mouths of hunger. One of them circled toward the humans' flank, the other crouched. Donovan yanked his sword clear.

"Get behind me," he snapped, turning to face the approaching hunter.

"No—back to back—" Helena's own blade rasped from its sheath. She lifted a shout for help.

The nearest animal sprung for her throat. She hacked wildly; the blade twisted in her hand and scraped the muzzled face. Jaws clamped on the edged steel and let go with a bloody howl. Donovan swung at the other beast, the blow shuddered home and it screamed and writhed and snapped at his ankles.

Whirling, he turned on the thing that had launched itself at Helena. He hewed, and the animal wasn't there, his blade rang on naked stone. A weight crashed against his back, he went down and the teeth damped on his shoulder.

Helena swung. The carnivore raised its head to snarl at her, and she gripped the sword in both hands and stabbed. It threshed wildly, dying, spewing blood over the hillside. The other wounded creature disappeared.

Helena bent over Donovan, held him close, her eyes wild. "Are you hurt? Basil. Oh Basil, are you hurt?"

"No," he muttered. "The teeth didn't have time to work through this heavy jacket." He pulled her head down against his.

"Basil, Basil!"

He rose, still holding her to him. Her arms locked about his neck, and there were tears and laughter in her voice. "Oh, Basil, my darling."

"Helena," he murmured. "I love you, Helena."

"When we get home—I'm due for furlough, I'll retire instead—your house on Ansa—Oh, Basil, I never thought I could be so glad!"

The massive thunder of feet brought them apart. Wocha burst around the thicket, swinging his giant ax in both hands. "Are you all right, boss?" he roared.

"Yes, yes, we're all right. A couple of those damned wolf-like things, which've been plaguing us the whole march. Go on back, Wocha, we'll join you soon."

The Donarrian's ape-face split in a vast grin. "So you take a female, boss?" he cried. "Good, good, we need lots of little Donovans at home!"

"Get on back, you old busybody, and keep that gossiping mouth shut!"

Hours later, Helena returned to the army where it was making camp. Donovan stayed where he was, looking down at the men where they moved about gathering wood and digging fire-pits. The blazes were a note of cheer in the thickening murk.

Helena, he thought. *Helena. She's a fine girl, wonderful girl, she's what the thinning Family blood and I, myself, need. But why did I do it? Why did I talk that way to her? Just then, in the strain and fear and loneliness, it seemed as if I cared. But I don't. She's just another woman. She's not Valduma.*

THE TWILIGHT murmured, and he saw the dim sheen of metal beside him. The men of Drogobych were gathering.

They stood tall and godlike in helmet and ring-mail and night-black cloaks, leaning on swords and spears, death-white faces cold with an ancient scorn as they looked down on the human camp. Their eyes were phosphorescent green in the dark.

Donovan nodded, without fear or surprise or anything but a sudden great weariness. He remembered some of them from the days when he had been alone in the bows of the ship with the invaders while his men cowered and rioted and went crazy in the stern sectors. "Hello, Morzach, Uboda, Zegoian, Korstuzan, Davleka," he said. "Welcome back again."

Valduma walked out of the blood-hued twilight, and he took her in his arms and held her for a long fierce time. Her kiss was as cruel as a swooping hawk. She bit his lips and he tasted blood warm and salt where she had been. Afterward she turned in the circle of his arm and they faced the silent men of Drogobych.

"You are getting near the city," said Morzach. His tones were deep, with the chill ringing of struck steel in them. "It is time for the next stage."

"I thought you saved some of us deliberately," said Donovan.

"*Us?*" Valduma's lips caressed his cheek. "Them, Basil, them. You don't belong there, you are with Arzun and me."

"You must have projected that game where we could spot it," went on Donovan, shakily. "You've kept us—them—alive and enabled us to march on your city—on the last inhabited city left to your race. You could have hunted them down as you did all the others, made sport of them with wild animals and falling rocks and missiles shooting out of nowhere, but instead you want them for something else. What is it?"

"You should have guessed," said Morzach. "We want to leave Arzun."

"Leave it? You can do so any time, by yourselves. You've done it for millennia."

"We can only go to the barbarian fringe stars. Beyond them it is a greater distance to the next suns than we can

48

cross unaided. Yet though we have captured many spaceships and have them intact at Drogobych, we cannot operate
them. The principles learned from the humans don't make
sense! When we have tried to pilot them, it has only brought
disaster."

"But why do you want to leave?"

"It is a recent decision, precipitated by your arrival, but it
has been considered for a long while. This sun is old, this
planet exhausted, and the lives of we few remnants of a great
race flicker in a hideous circumscribed drabness. Sooner or
later, the humans will fight their way here in strength too
great for us. Before then we must be gone."

"So..." Donovan spoke softly, and the wind whimpered
under his voice. "So your plan is to capture this group of
spacemen and make them your slaves, to carry you where?"

"Out. Away." Valduma's clear lovely laughter rang in the
night. "To seize another planet and build our strength
afresh," She gripped his waist and he saw the white gleam of
her teeth out of shadow. "To build a great army of obedient
space-going warriors—and then out to hunt between the
stars!"

"Look here." Morzach edged closer, his eyes a green
glow, the vague sheen of naked steel in his hand. "I've been
polite long enough. You have your chance, to rise above the
human scum that spawned you and be one of us. Help us
now and you can be with us till you die. Otherwise, we'll take
that crew anyway, and you'll be hounded across the face of
this planet."

*"Aye—aye—welcome back, Basil Donovan, welcome back to the
old king-race... Come with us, come with us, lead the humans into our
ambush and be the lord of stars..."*

They circled about him, tall and beautiful in the shadow-
light, luring whispering voices, ripple of dark laughter, the
hunters playing with their quarry and taming it. Donovan

remembered them, remembered the days when he had talked and smiled and drunk and sung with them, the Lucifer-like intoxication of their dancing darting minds, a wildness of magic and mystery and reckless wizard sport, a glory that had taken something from his soul and left an emptiness within him. Morzach, Marovech, Uboda, Zegoian, for a time he had been the consort of the gods.

"Basil." Valduma laid sharp-nailed fingers in his hair and pulled his lips to hers. "Basil, I want you back."

He held her close, feeling the lithe savage strength of her, recalling the flame-like beauty and the nights of love such as no human could ever give. His whisper was thick: "You got bored last time and sent me back. How long will I last now?"

"As long as you wish. Basil. Forever and forever." He knew she lied, and he didn't care.

"This is what you must do, Donovan," said Morzach.

He listened with half his mind. It was a question of guiding the army into a narrow cul-de-sac where the Arzunians could perform the delicate short-range work of causing chains to bind around them. For the rest, he was thinking.

They hunt. They intrigue, and they whittle down their last few remnants with fighting among themselves, and they prey on the fringe stars, and they capture living humans to hunt down for sport. They haven't done anything new for ten thousand years, creativeness has withered from them, and all they will do if they escape the Nebula is carry ruin between the stars. They're mad.

Yes—a whole society of psychopaths, gone crazy with the long racial dying. That's the real reason they can't handle machines; that's why they don't think of friendship but only of war; that's why they carry doom within them.

But I love you, I love you, I love you, O Valduma the fair.

He drew her to him, kissed her with a terrible intensity, and she laughed in the dark. Looking up, he faced the blaze that was Morzach.

"All right," he said. "I understand. Tomorrow."

"Aye—good, good, well done!"

"Oh, Basil, Basil!" whispered Valduma. "Come, come away with me, now."

"No. They'd suspect. I have to go down to them or they'll come looking for me."

"Good night, Basil, my darling, my vorza. Until tomorrow…"

He went slowly down the hillside, drawing his shoulders together against the cold, not looking back. Helena rose when he approached her campfire, and the flimmering light made her seem pale and unreal.

"Where have you been, Basil? You look so tired."

"Just walking around. I'm all right." He spread his couch of stiff and stinking animal hides. "We'd better turn in, eh?"

But he slept little.

CHAPTER SIX

THE HIGHWAY curved between great looming walls of cragged old rock, a shadow tunnel with the wind yowling far overhead and the sun a disc of blood. Men's footfalls echoed from the cracked paving blocks to boom hollowly off time-gnawed cliffs and ring faintly in the ice. It was cold, their breath smoked from them and they shivered and cursed and stamped their feet.

Donovan walked beside Helena, who was riding Wocha. His eyes narrowed against the searching wind, looking ahead and around, looking for the side track where the ambush waited. Drogobych was very near.

Something moved up on the ridge, a flapping black thing, which was instantly lost to sight. The Arzunians were watching.

There—up ahead—the solitary tree they had spoken of, growing out between age-crumbled fragments of the road. The highway swung west around a pinnacle of rock, but here there was a branch road running straight south into a narrow ravine. *All I have to do is suggest we take it. They won't know till too late that it leads up to a blind canyon.*

Helena leaned over toward him, so that the long wind-whipped hair blew against his cheek. "Which way should we go?" she asked. One hand rested on his shoulder.

He didn't slacken his stride, but his voice was low under the whine of bitter air: "To the right, Helena, and on the double. The Arzunians are waiting up the other road, but Drogobych is just beyond that crag."

"Basil! How do you know—"

Wocha's long hairy ears cocked attentively, and the little eyes under the heavy bone ridges were suddenly sharp on his master.

"They wanted me to mislead you. I didn't say anything before for fear they'd be listening, somehow."

Because I hadn't decided, he thought gravely. Because Valduma is mad, and I love her.

Helena turned and lifted her arm, voice ringing out to rattle in jeering echoes: "Column right! Forward—charge!"

Wocha broke into a trot, the ground booming and shivering under his huge feet. Donovan paced beside, drawing his sword and swinging it naked in one hand, his eyes turned to the canyon and the rocks above it. The humans fell into a jogging run.

They swept past the ambush road, and suddenly Valduma was on the ridge above them, tall and slim and beautiful, the hair like a blowing flame under her helmet. "Basil!" she screamed. "Basil, you triple traitor—"

The others were there with her, men of Drogobych standing on the heights and howling their fury. They had chains in their hands, and suddenly the air was thick with flying links.

One of them smashed against Donovan and curled itself snake-like around his waist. He dropped his sword and tugged at the cold iron, feeling the breath strained out of him, cursing with the pain of it. Wocha reached down a hand and peeled the chain off, snapping it in two and hurling it back at the Arzunians. It whipped in the air, lashing itself across his face, and he bellowed.

The men of Sol were weltering in a fight with the flying chains, beating them off, stamping the writhing lengths underfoot, yelling as the things cracked against their heads.

"Forward!" cried Helena. "Charge—get out of here—forward, Empire!"

A chain whistled viciously for her face. She struck at it with her sword, tangling it on the blade, metal clashing on metal. Takahashi had his blaster out, its few remaining charges thundering to fuse the missiles. Other flames roared at the Arzunians, driving them back, forcing them to drop control of the chains to defend their lives.

"Run! Forward!"

The column shouted and plunged down the highway. Valduma was suddenly before them, her face distorted in fury, stabbing a spear at Donovan's breast. The man parried the thrust and hewed at her—she was gone, and the Terrans rushed ahead.

The rocks groaned. Donovan saw them shuddering above him, saw the first hail of gravel and heard the huge grinding of strata. "They're trying to bury us!" he yelled. "We've got to get clear!"

Wocha stooped, snatched him up under one arm, and galloped. A boulder whizzed by his head, smashing against the farther wall and spraying him with hot chips of stone. Now the boom of the landslide filled their world, rolling and roaring between the high cliffs. Cracks zigzagged across the worn black heights; the crags shivered and toppled, dust boiled across the road.

"Basil!"

Donovan saw Valduma again, dancing and leaping between the boulders, raising a scream of wrath and laughter. Morzach was there, standing on a jut of rock, watching the hillside fall.

Wocha burst around the sentinel peak. A line of Arzunians stood barring the way to Drogobych, the sunlight flaming off their metal. Wocha dropped Donovan, hefted his ax in both hands, and charged them.

Donovan picked himself up and scrambled in the wake of his slave. Behind him, the Terrans were streaming from the collapsing dale, out over open ground to strike the enemy. The rocks bounded and howled, a man screamed as he was pinned, there were a dozen buried under the landslide.

Wocha hit the Arzunian line. His ax blazed, shearing off an arm, whirling up again to crumple a helmet and cleave the skull beneath. Rearing, he knocked down two of them and trampled them underfoot. A warrior smote at his flank. Helena, gripping one mighty shoulder, engaged him with her free hand, her blade whistling around his ears. They fell away from that pair, and the Terrans attacked them.

DONOVAN CROSSED swords with someone he knew—Marovech, the laughing half-devil whose words he had so much enjoyed in earlier days. The Arzunian grinned at him across a web of flying steel. His blade stabbed in, past the Ansan's awkward guard, reaching for his guts. Donovan retreated, abandoning the science he didn't know for a wild whirling and hacking, his iron battering at the bright weapon before him. Clash and clang of edged metal, leaping and dancing, Marovech's red hair wild in the rising wind and his eyes alight with laughter.

Donovan felt his backward step halted, he was against the high stone pillar and could not run. He braced his feet and hewed out, a scream of cloven air and outraged steel. Marovech's sword went spinning from his hand.

It hit the ground and bounced up toward the Arzunian's clutch. Donovan smote again, and the shock of iron in flesh jarred him where he stood. Marovech fell in a rush of blood.

For an instant Donovan stood swaying over the Arzunian, looking stupidly at the blood on his own hands, hearing the clamor of his heartbeat and sucking a dry gasp into his lungs.

Then he picked up the fallen being's glaive, a deadly pole-sword. It was a better weapon.

Turning, he saw that the fight had become a riot, knots of men and un-men snarling and hacking in a craziness of death. No room or time here for wizard stunts, it was blood and bone and nerve against its kind. The Terrans fought without much skill in the use of their archaic equipment but they had the cold courage blended of training and desperation. And they knew better how to cooperate. They battled a way to each other and stood back to back against all comers.

Wocha raged and trampled, smashing with ax and fist and feet and hurled stones, his war cry bellowing and shuddering in the hills. An Arzunian vanished from in front of him and appeared behind with spear poised. The Donarrian suddenly backed up, catching the assailant and smashing him under his hind feet while he dueled another from the front. Helena's arm never rested, she swung to right and left, guarding his flanks yelling as her blade drove home.

Donovan shook himself and trotted warily over to where a tide of Arzunians raged about a closely drawn ring of Impies. The humans were standing firm, driving each charge back in a rush of blood, heaping the dead before them. But now spears were beginning to fall out of the sky, driven by no hand but stabbing for the throats and eyes and bellies of men. Donovan loped for the sharp edge of the hills, where they toppled to the open country in which the fight went on.

He scrambled up a rubbled slope and gripped a thin pinnacle to swing himself higher. She was there.

She stood on a ledge, the heap of spears lit her feet, looking down over the battle and chanting as she sent forth the flying death. He noticed even then how her hair was a red glory about the fine white loveliness of her head.

"Valduma," he whispered, as he struck at her.

She was not there; she sat on a higher ledge and jeered at him. "Come and get me, Basil, darling, darling. Come up here and talk to me!"

He looked at her as Lucifer must have looked back to Heaven. "Let us go," he said. "Give us a ship and send us home."

"And have you bring our overlords back in?" She laughed aloud.

"They aren't so bad, Valduma. The Empire means peace and justice for all races."

"Who speaks?" Her scorn flamed at him. "You don't believe that."

He stood there for a moment. "No," he whispered. "No, I don't."

Stooping, he picked up the sheaf of spears and began to crawl back down the rocks. Valduma cursed him from the heights.

There was a break in the combat around the hard-pressed Terran ring as the Arzunians drew back to pant and glare. Donovan ran through and flung his load clashing at the feet of Takahashi.

"Good work," said the officer. "We need these things. Here, get into the formation. Here we go again!"

The Arzunians charged in a wedge to gather momentum. Donovan braced himself and lifted his sword. The Terrans in the inner ring slanted their spears between the men of the outer defense. For a very long half-minute, they stood waiting.

The enemy hit! Donovan hewed at the nearest, drove the probing sword back and hammered against the guard. Then the whirl of battle swept his antagonist away, someone else was there, he traded blows and the howl of men and metal lifted skyward.

The Terrans had staggered a little from the massive assault, but it spitted itself on the inner pikes and then swords and axes went to work. Ha, clang, through the skull and give it to 'em! Hai, Empire! Ansa, Ansa! Clatter and yell and deep-throated roar, the Arzunians boiling around the Solar line, leaping and howling and whipping out of sight—a habit that saved their lives but blunted their attack, thought Donovan in a moment's pause.

Wocha smashed the last few who had been standing before him, looked around to the major struggle, and pawed the ground. "Ready lady?" he rumbled.

"Aye, ready, Wocha," cried Helena. "Let's go!"

The Donarrian backed up to get a long running space. "Hang on tight," he warned. "Never mind fighting, lady. All right!"

He broke into a trot, a canter, and then a full gallop. The earth trembled under his mass. Hoooo!" he screamed. "Here we come!"

Helena threw both arms around his corded neck. When they hit it was like a nuclear bomb going off.

In a few seconds of murder, Wocha had strewn the ground with smashed corpses, whirled and begun cutting his way into the disordered main group of the Arzunians. They didn't stand before him. Suddenly they were gone, all of them, except for the dead.

Donovan looked over the field. The dead were thick, thick. He estimated that half the little Terran force was slain or out of action. But they must have taken three or four times their number of Arzunians to the Black Planet with them. The stony ground was pooled and steaming with blood. Carrion birds stooped low, screaming.

Helena fell from Wocha's back into Donovan's arms. He comforted her wild sobbing, holding her to him and murmuring in her ear and kissing the wet cheeks and lips. "It's over, dear, it's over for now. We drove them away."

She recovered herself in a while and stood up, straightening her torn disarray, the mask of command clamping back over her face. To Takahashi: "How are our casualties?"

He reported. It was much as Donovan had guessed. "But we gave 'em hell for it, didn't we?"

"How is that?" wondered Cohen. He leaned against Wocha, not showing the pain that jagged through him as they bandaged his wounded foot except by an occasional sharp breath. "They're more at home with this cutlery than we, and they have those damned parapsych talents too."

"They're not quite sane," replied Donovan tonelessly. "Whether you call it a cultural trait or a madness that has spread to the whole population, they're a wild bloodthirsty crew, two-legged weasels, and with a superiority complex that wouldn't have let them be very careful in dealing with us. No discipline, no real plan of action." He looked south over the rolling moorland. "Those things count. They may know better next time."

"Next time? Fifty or sixty men can't defeat a planet, Donovan," said Takahashi.

"No. Though this is an old dying race, their whole population in the city ahead, and most of it will flee in panic and take no part in any fighting. They aren't used to victims that fight back. If we can slug our way through to the spaceships they have there—"

"Spaceships!" The eyes stared at him, wild with a sudden blaze of hope, men crowding close and leaning on their reddened weapons and raising a babble of voices: *"Spaceships, spaceships—home!"*

"Yeah." Donovan ran a hand through his yellow hair. The fingers trembled just a bit. "Some ships, the first ones, they merely destroyed by causing the engines to run loose; but others they brought here, I suppose, by inducing the crew to land and parley. Only they killed the crews and can't handle the machines themselves."

"If they captured ships," said Helena slowly, "then they captured weapons too, and even they can squeeze a trigger."

"Sure. But you didn't see them shooting at us just now, did you? They used all the charges to hunt or duel. So if we can break through and escape—"

"They could still follow us and wreck our engines," said Takahashi.

"Not if we take a small ship, as we'd have to anyway, and mount guard over the vital spots. An Arzunian would have to be close at hand and using all his energies to misdirect atomic flows. He could be killed before any mischief was done. I doubt if they'd even try.

"Besides," went on Donovan, his voice dry and toneless as a lecturing professor's, "they can only do so much at a time. I don't know where they get the power for some of their feats, such as leaving this planet's gravitational well. It can't be from their own metabolisms, it must be some unknown cosmic energy source. They don't know how it works themselves; it's an instinctive ability. But it takes a lot of nervous energy to direct that flow, and I found last time I was here that they have to rest quite a while after some strenuous deed. So if we can get them tired enough—and the fight is likely to wear both sides down—they won't be able to chase us till we're out of their range."

Takahashi looked oddly at him. "You know a lot," he murmured.

"Yeah, maybe I do."

"Well, if the city is close as you say, we'd better march right away before our wounds stiffen, and before the natives get a chance to organize."

SARGASSO OF LOST STARSHIPS

"Rig up carrying devices for those too badly hurt to move," said Helena. "The walking wounded can tote them, and the rest of us form a protective square."

"Won't that slow us and handicap us?" asked Donovan.

Her head lifted, the golden hair blowing about her proud features in the thin whimpering wind. "As long as it's humanly possible we're going to look after our men. What's the Imperium for if it can't protect it's own?"

"Yeah. Yeah, I suppose so."

Donovan slouched off to join the salvaging party that was stripping the fallen Arzunians of arms and armor for Terran use. He rolled over a corpse to unbuckle the helmet and looked at the blood-masked face of Korstuzan who had been his friend once, very long ago. He closed the staring eyes, and his own were blind with tears.

Wocha came to join him. The Donarrian didn't seem to notice the gashes in his hide, but he was equipped with a shield now and had a couple of extra swords slung from his shoulders. "You got a good lady, boss," he said. "She fights hard. She will bear you strong sons."

"Uh-huh."

Valduma could never bear my children. Different species can't breed. And she is the outlaw darkness, the last despairing return to primeval chaos, she is the enemy of all which is honest and good. But she is very fair.

Slowly, the humans reformed their army, a tight ring about their wounded, and set off down the road. The dim sun wheeled horizonward.

CHAPTER SEVEN

DROGOBYCH lay before them.

The city stood on the open gray moor, and it had once been large. But its outer structures were long crumbled to ruin, heaps and shards of stone riven by ages of frost, fallen and covered by the creeping dust. Here and there a squared monolith remained like the last snag in a rotted jaw, dark against the windy sky. It was quiet. Nothing stirred in all the sweeping immensity of hill and moor and ruin and loneliness.

Helena pointed from her seat on Wocha, and a lilt of hope was eager in the tired voice: "See—a ship—ahead there!"

They stared, and someone raised a ragged cheer. Over the black square-built houses of the inner city they could make out the metal nose of a freighter. Takahashi squinted. "It's Denebian, I think," he said. "Looks as if man isn't the only race that has suffered from these scum."

"All right, boys," said Helena. "Let's go in and get it."

They went down a long empty avenue, which ran spear-straight for the Center. The porticoed houses gaped with wells of blackness at their passage, looming in cracked and crazily leaning massiveness on either side, throwing back the hollow slam of their boots. Donovan heard the uneasy mutter of voices to his rear: *Don't like this place... Haunted... They could be waiting anywhere for us..."*

The wind blew a whirl of snow across their path.

Basil. Basil, my dear.

Donovan's head jerked around, and he felt his throat tighten. Nothing. No movement, no sound, emptiness.

Basil, I am calling you. No one else can hear.

Why are you with these creatures, Basil? Why are you marching with the oppressors of your planet? We could free Ansa, Basil, given time to raise our armies. We could sweep the Terrans before us and hound them down the ways of night. And yet you march against us.

"Valduma," he whispered.

Basil, you were very dear to me. You were something new and strong and of the future, come to our weary old world, and I think I loved you.

I could still love you, Basil. I could hold you forever, if you would let me.

"Valduma—have done!"

A mocking ripple of laughter, sweet as rain in springtime, the gallantry of a race that was old and sick and doomed and could still know mirth. Donovan shook his head and stared rigidly before him. It was as if he had laid hands on that piece of his soul that had been lost, and she was trying to wrench it from him again. Only he wanted her to win.

Go home, Basil. Go home with this female of yours. Breed your cubs, fill the home with brats, and try to think your little round of days means something. Strut about under the blue skies, growing fat and gray, bragging of what a great fellow you used to be and disapproving of the younger generation. As you like, Basil. But don't go out to space again. Don't look at the naked stars. You won't dare.

"No," he whispered.

She laughed, a harsh bell of mockery ringing in his brain. *You could have been a god—or a devil. But you would rather be a pot-bellied Imperial magistrate. Go home, Basil Donovan, take your female home, and when you are wakened at night by her—shall we say her breathing—do not remember me.*

The Terrans slogged on down the street, filthy with dust and grease and blood, uncouth shamblers, apes in the somber ruin of the gods. Donovan thought he had a glimpse of Valduma standing on a rooftop, the clean lithe fire of her, silken flame of her hair and the green unhuman eyes, which had lighted in the dark at his side. She had been a living blaze, an unending trumpet and challenge, and when she broke with him it had been quick and clean, no soddenness of age and custom and—and, damn it, all the little things that made humanness.

All right, Valduma. We're monkeys. We're noisy and self-important, compromisers and trimmers and petty cheats, we huddle away from the greatness we could have, our edifices are laid brick by brick with endless futile squabbling over each one—and yet, Valduma, there is something in man that you don't have. There's something by which these men have fought their way through everything you could loose on them, helping each other, going forward under a ridiculous rag of colored cloth and singing as they went.

Fine words, added his mind. *Too bad you don't really believe them.*

He grew aware of Helena's anxious eyes on him. "What's the matter, darling?" she asked gently. "You look ill."

"Tired," he said. "But we can't have so very far to go now—"

"Look out!"

Whirling, he saw the pillars of the house to the right buckle, saw the huge stone slabs of the roof come thundering over the top and streetward. For a blinding instant he saw Valduma, riding the slab down, yelling and laughing, and then she was gone and the stone struck.

They were already running, dropping their burden of the hurt and fleeing for safety. Another house groaned and rumbled. The ground shook, flying shards stung Donovan's back, echoes rolled down the ways of Drogobych. Someone was screaming, far and faint under the grinding racket.

"Forward. Forward!" Helena's voice whipped back to him; she led the rush while the city thundered about her. Then a veil of rising dust blotted her out, he groped ahead, stumbling over fallen pillars and cornices, hearing the boom around him, running and running.

Valduma laughed, a red flame through the whirling dust. Her spear gleamed for his breast; he grabbed it with one hand and hacked at her with his sword. She was gone, and he raced ahead, not stopping to think, not daring.

They came out on a great open plaza. Once there had been a park here, and carved fountains, but nothing remained save a few leafless trees and broken pieces.

And the spaceships.

THE spaceships, a loom of metal against the dark stone beyond, half a dozen standing there and waiting—spaceships, spaceships, the most beautiful sight in the cosmos! Helena and Wocha were halted near a small fast Comet-class scoutboat. The surviving Terrans ran toward them. Few, thought Donovan sickly, few—perhaps a score left, bleeding from the cuts of flying stone, gray with dust and fear. The city had been a trap.

"Come on!" yelled the woman. "Over here and off this planet!"

The men of Drogobych were suddenly there, a ring about the ship and another about the whole plaza, crouched with their weapons and their cat's eyes aflame. A score, of hurt starvelings and half a thousand un-men.

A trumpet blew its high note into the dusking heavens. The Arzunians rested arms, expressionless. Donovan and the other humans continued their pace, forming a battle square.

Morzach stood forth in front of the scoutship. "You have no further chance to escape," he called. "But we want your services, not your lives, and the service will be well rewarded. Lay down your weapons."

Wocha's arm straightened. His ax flew like a thunderbolt, and Morzach's head burst open. The Donarrian roared and went against the enemy line.

They edged away, fearfully, and the Terrans followed him in a trotting wedge. Donovan moved up on Wocha's right side, sword hammering at the thrusts for his ribs.

An Arzunian yelled an order that must have meant, "Stop them!" Donovan saw the outer line break into a run, converging on the knot of struggle. No flying spears this time, he reflected in a moment's bleak satisfaction—tearing down those walls must have exhausted most of their directing energies.

A native rushed at him, sword whistling from behind a black shield. Donovan caught the blow on his own plundered scute, feeling it ring in the bones of his arm, and hewed back. His blade screamed close to the white teeth-bared face, and he called a panting salutation: "Try again, Davleka!"

"I will!"

The blows rained on his shield, sang viciously low to cut at his legs, clattering and clanging, whistle of air and howl of iron under the westering sun. He backed up against Wocha's side, where the Donarrian and the woman smote against the airlock's defenders, and braced himself and struck out.

Davleka snarled and hacked at Donovan's spread leg. The Ansan's glaive snaked forth against his unshielded neck. Davleka's sword clashed to earth and he sprawled against the human. Raising his bloody face, he drew a knife, lifted it, and tried to thrust upward. Donovan, already crossing blades with Uboda, stamped on his hand. Davleka grinned, a rueful crooked grin through the streaming blood, and died.

Uboda pressed close, working up against Donovan's shield. He had none himself, but there was a dirk in his left hand. His sword locked with Donovan's, strained it aside, and his knife clattered swiftly for an opening.

Helena turned about and struck from her seat. Uboda's head rolled against Donovan's shield and left a red splash down it. The man retched.

Wocha, swinging one of his swords, pushed ahead into the Arzunians, crowding them aside by his sheer mass, beating down a guard and the helmet or armor beyond it. "Clear!" he bellowed. I got the way clear, lady!"

Helena sprang to the ground and into the leek. "Takahashi, Cohen, Basil, Wang-ki, come in and help me start the engines. The rest of you hold them off. Don't give them time to exert what collective para power they have left and ruin something. Make them think!"

"Think about their lives, huh?" Wocha squared off in front of the airlock and raised his sword. "All right, boys, here they come. Let 'em have what they want."

Donovan halted in the airlock. Valduma was there, her fiery head whirling in the rash of black-clad warriors. He leaned over and grabbed a spaceman's aim. "Ben Ali, go in and help start this crate. I have to stay here."

"But—"

Donovan shoved him in, stood beside Takahashi, and braced himself to meet the Arzunian charge.

They rushed in, knowing that they had to kill the humans before there was an escape, swinging their weapons and howling. The shock of the assault threw men back, pressed them to the ship and jammed weapons close to breasts. The Terrans cursed and began to use fists and feet, clearing a space to fight in.

Donovan's sword clashed against a shield, drove off another blade, stabbed for a face, and then it was all lost in the crazed maelstrom, hack and thrust and take the blows they give, hew, sword, hew!

They raged against Wocha, careless now of their lives, thundering blows against his shield, slashing and stabbing and using then last wizard strength to fill the air with blades. He roared and stood his ground, the sword leaped in his hand, metal clove in thunder. The shield was crumpled, falling apart—he tossed it with rib-cracking force against the nearest Arzunian. His nicked and blunted sword burst against a helmet, and he drew the other.

The ship trembled, thutter of engines warming up, the eager promise of sky and stars and green Terra again. "Get in!" bawled Donovan. "Get in! We'll hold them!"

He stood by Wocha as the last crewmen entered, stood barring the airlock with a wall of blood and iron. Through a blurring vision, he saw Valduma approach.

She smiled at him, one slim hand running through the copper hair, the other held out in sign of peace. Tall and gracious and lovely beyond his knowing, she moved up toward Donovan, and her clear voice rang in his darkening mind.

Basil—you, at least, could stay. You could guide us out to the stars.

"You go away," groaned Wocha.

The devil's rage flamed in her face. She yelled, and a lance whistled from the sky and buried itself in the great breast.

"Wocha!" yelled Donovan.

The Donarrian snarled and snipped off the shaft that stood between his ribs. He whirled it over his head, and Valduma's green eyes widened in fear.

"Donovan!" roared Wocha, and let it fly.

It smashed home, and the Ansan dropped his sword and swayed on his feet. He couldn't look on the broken thing that had been Valduma.

"Boss, you go home now."

Wocha laid him in the airlock and then slammed the outer valve shut. Turning, he faced the Arzunians. He couldn't see very well—one eye was gone, and there was a ragged darkness before the other. The sword felt heavy in his hand. But—

"Hooo!" he roared and charged them. He spitted one and trampled another and tossed a third into the air. Whirling, he dove a head and smashed a rib-case with his fist and chopped another across. His sword broke, and he grabbed two Arzunians and cracked their skulls together.

They ran, then, turned and fled from him. And he stood watching them go and laughed. His laughter filled the city, rolling from its walls, drowning the whistle of the ship's takeoff and bringing blood to his lips. He wiped his mouth with the back of one hand, spat, and lay down.

"WE'RE CLEAR, Basil." Helena clung to him, shivering in his arms, and he didn't know if it was a laugh or a sob in her throat. "We're away, safe, we'll carry word back to Sol and they'll clear the Black Nebula for good."

"Yeah." He rubbed his eyes. "Though I doubt the Navy will find anything. If those Arzunians have any sense, they'll project to various fringe planets, scatter, and try to pass as harmless humanoids. But it doesn't matter, I suppose. Their power is broken."

"And we'll go back to your home, Basil, and bring Ansa and Terra together and have a dozen children and..."

He nodded. "Sure. Sure..."

But he wouldn't forget. In the winter nights, when the stars were sharp and cold in a sky of ringing crystal black, he would—go out and watch them? Or pull his roof over him and wait for dawn? He didn't know yet.

Still—even if this was a long ways from being the best of all possible universes, it had enough in it to make a man glad of his day.

He whistled softly, feeling the words run through his head:

Lift your glasses high,
kiss the girls goodbye,
  (Live well, my friend, live well, live you well)
for we're riding,
for we're riding,
for we're riding out to Terran sky! Terran sky! Terran sky!

The thought came all at once that it could be a song of comradeship, too.

THE END

If you've enjoyed this book, you will not want to miss these terrific titles…

ARMCHAIR SCI-FI, FANTASY, & HORROR DOUBLE NOVELS, $12.95 each

D-41 **FULL CYCLE** by Clifford D. Simak
IT WAS THE DAY OF THE ROBOT by Frank Belknap Long

D-42 **THIS CROWDED EARTH** by Robert Bloch
REIGN OF THE TELEPUPPETS by Daniel Galouye

D-43 **THE CRISPIN AFFAIR** by Jack Sharkey
THE RED HELL OF JUPITER by Paul Ernst

D-44 **PLANET OF DREAD** by Dwight V. Swain
WE THE MACHINE by Gerald Vance

D-45 **THE STAR HUNTER** by Edmond Hamilton
THE ALIEN by Raymond F. Jones

D-46 **WORLD OF IF** by Rog Phillips
SLAVE RAIDERS FROM MERCURY by Don Wilcox

D-47 **THE ULTIMATE PERIL** by Robert Abernathy
PLANET OF SHAME by Bruce Elliot

D-48 **THE FLYING EYES** by J. Hunter Holly
SOME FABULOUS YONDER by Phillip Jose Farmer

D-49 **THE COSMIC BUNGLERS** by Geoff St. Reynard
THE BUTTONED SKY by Geoff St. Reynard

D-50 **TYRANTS OF TIME** by Milton Lesser
PARIAH PLANET by Murray Leinster

ARMCHAIR SCIENCE FICTION CLASSICS, $12.95 each

C-13 **SUNKEN WORLD**
by Stanton A. Coblentz

C-14 **THE LAST VIAL**
by Sam McClatchie, M. D.

C-15 **WE WHO SURVIVED (THE FIFTH ICE AGE)**
by Sterling Noel

ARMCHAIR MASTERS OF SCIENCE FICTION SERIES, $16.95 each

MS-5 **MASTERS OF SCIENCE FICTION, Vol. Five**
Winston K. Marks—Test Colony and other tales

MS-6 **MASTERS OF SCIENCE FICTION, Vol. Six**
Fritz Leiber—Deadly Moon and other tales

If you've enjoyed this book, you will not want to miss these terrific titles…

ARMCHAIR SCI-FI & HORROR DOUBLE NOVELS, $12.95 each

D-51   **A GOD NAMED SMITH** by Henry Slesar
WORLDS OF THE IMPERIUM by Keith Laumer

D-52   **CRAIG'S BOOK** by Don Wilcox
EDGE OF THE KNIFE by H. Beam Piper

D-53   **THE SHINING CITY** by Rena M. Vale
THE RED PLANET by Russ Winterbotham

D-54   **THE MAN WHO LIVED TWICE** by Rog Phillips
VALLEY OF THE CROEN by Lee Tarbell

D-55   **OPERATION DISASTER** by Milton Lesser
LAND OF THE DAMNED by Berkeley Livingston

D-56   **CAPTIVE OF THE CENTAURIANESS** by Poul Anderson
A PRINCESS OF MARS by Edgar Rice Burroughs

D-57   **THE NON-STATISTICAL MAN** by Raymond F. Jones
MISSION FROM MARS by Rick Conroy

D-58   **INTRUDERS FROM THE STARS** by Ross Rocklynne
FLIGHT OF THE STARLING by Chester S. Geier

D-59   **COSMIC SABOTEUR** by Frank M. Robinson
LOOK TO THE STARS by Willard Hawkins

D-60   **THE MOON IS HELL!** by John W. Campbell, Jr.
THE GREEN WORLD by Hal Clement

ARMCHAIR SCIENCE FICTION CLASSICS, $12.95 each

C-16   **THE SHAVER MYSTERY, Book Three**
by Richard S. Shaver

C-17   **THE PLANET STRAPPERS**
by Raymond Z. Gallun

C-18   **THE FOURTH "R"**
by George O. Smith

ARMCHAIR SCIENCE FICTION & HORROR GEMS SERIES, $12.95 each

G-5   **SCIENCE FICTION GEMS, Vol. Three**
C. M. Kornbluth and others

G-6   **HORROR GEMS, Vol. Three**
August Derleth and others

If you've enjoyed this book, you will not want to miss these terrific titles...

ARMCHAIR SCI-FI & HORROR DOUBLE NOVELS, $12.95 each

D-61 **THE MAN WHO STOPPED AT NOTHING** by Paul W. Fairman
TEN FROM INFINITY by Ivar Jorgensen

D-62 **WORLDS WITHIN** by Rog Phillips
THE SLAVE by C.M. Kornbluth

D-63 **SECRET OF THE BLACK PLANET** by Milton Lesser
THE OUTCASTS OF SOLAR III by Emmett McDowell

D-64 **WEB OF THE WORLDS** by Harry Harrison and Katherine MacLean
RULE GOLDEN by Damon Knight

D-65 **TEN TO THE STARS** by Raymond Z. Gallun
THE CONQUERORS by David H. Keller, M. D.

D-66 **THE HORDE FROM INFINITY** by Dwight V. Swain
THE DAY THE EARTH FROZE by Gerald Hatch

D-67 **THE WAR OF THE WORLDS** by H. G. Wells
THE TIME MACHINE by H. G. Wells

D-68 **STARCOMBERS** by Edmond Hamilton
THE YEAR WHEN STARDUST FELL by Raymond F. Jones

D-69 **HOCUS-POCUS UNIVERSE** by Jack Williamson
QUEEN OF THE PANTHER WORLD by Berkeley Livingston

D-70 **BATTERING RAMS OF SPACE** by Don Wilcox
DOOMSDAY WING by George H. Smith

ARMCHAIR SCIENCE FICTION & FANTASY CLASSICS, $12.95 each

C-19 **EMPIRE OF JEGGA**
by David V. Reed

C-20 **THE TOMORROW PEOPLE**
by Judith Merril

C-21 **THE MAN FROM YESTERDAY**
by Howard Browne as by Lee Francis

C-22 **THE TIME TRADERS**
by Andre Norton

C-23 **ISLANDS OF SPACE**
by John W. Campbell

C-24 **THE GALAXY PRIMES**
by E. E. "Doc" Smith

If you've enjoyed this book, you will not want to miss these terrific titles…

ARMCHAIR SCI-FI & HORROR DOUBLE NOVELS, $12.95 each

D-71   **THE DEEP END** by Gregory Luce
TO WATCH BY NIGHT by Robert Moore Williams

D-72   **SWORDSMAN OF LOST TERRA** by Poul Anderson
PLANET OF GHOSTS by David V. Reed

D-73   **MOON OF BATTLE** by J. J. Allerton
THE MUTANT WEAPON by Murray Leinster

D-74   **OLD SPACEMEN NEVER DIE!** John Jakes
RETURN TO EARTH by Bryan Berry

D-75   **THE THING FROM UNDERNEATH** by Milton Lesser
OPERATION INTERSTELLAR by George O. Smith

D-76   **THE BURNING WORLD** by Algis Budrys
FOREVER IS TOO LONG by Chester S. Geier

D-77   **THE COSMIC JUNKMAN** by Rog Phillips
THE ULTIMATE WEAPON by John W. Campbell

D-78   **THE TIES OF EARTH** by James H. Schmitz
CUE FOR QUIET by Thomas L. Sherred

D-79   **SECRET OF THE MARTIANS** by Paul W. Fairman
THE VARIABLE MAN by Philip K. Dick

D-80   **THE GREEN GIRL** by Jack Williamson
THE ROBOT PERIL by Don Wilcox

ARMCHAIR SCIENCE FICTION CLASSICS, $12.95 each

C-25   **THE STAR KINGS**
by Edmond Hamilton

C-26   **NOT IN SOLITUDE**
by Kenneth Gantz

C-32   **PROMETHEUS II**
by S. J. Byrne

ARMCHAIR SCIENCE FICTION & HORROR GEMS SERIES, $12.95 each

G-7   **SCIENCE FICTION GEMS, Vol. Four**
Jack Sharkey and others

G-8   **HORROR GEMS, Vol. Four**
Seabury Quinn and others

If you've enjoyed this book, you will not want to miss these terrific titles…

ARMCHAIR SCI-FI, FANTASY, & HORROR DOUBLE NOVELS, $12.95 each

D-81 **THE LAST PLEA** by Robert Bloch
THE STATUS CIVILIZATION by Robert Sheckley

D-82 **WOMAN FROM ANOTHER PLANET** by Frank Belknap Long
HOMECALLING by Judith Merril

D-83 **WHEN TWO WORLDS MEET** by Robert Moore Williams
THE MAN WHO HAD NO BRAINS by Jeff Sutton

D-84 **THE SPECTRE OF SUICIDE SWAMP** by E. K. Jarvis
IT'S MAGIC, YOU DOPE! by Jack Sharkey

D-85 **THE STARSHIP FROM SIRIUS** by Rog Phillips
FINAL WEAPON by Everett Cole

D-86 **TREASURE ON THUNDER MOON** by Edmond Hamilton
TRAIL OF THE ASTROGAR by Henry Haase

D-87 **THE VENUS ENIGMA** by Joe Gibson
THE WOMAN IN SKIN 13 by Paul W. Fairman

D-88 **THE MAD ROBOT** by William P. McGivern
THE RUNNING MAN by J. Holly Hunter

D-89 **VENGEANCE OF KYVOR** by Randall Garrett
AT THE EARTH'S CORE by Edgar Rice Burroughs

D-90 **DWELLERS OF THE DEEP** by Don Wilcox
NIGHT OF THE LONG KNIVES by Fritz Leiber

ARMCHAIR SCIENCE FICTION CLASSICS, $12.95 each

C-28 **THE MAN FROM TOMORROW**
by Stanton A. Coblentz

C-29 **THE GREEN MAN OF GRAYPEC**
by Festus Pragnell

C-30 **THE SHAVER MYSTERY, Book Four**
by Richard S. Shaver

ARMCHAIR MASTERS OF SCIENCE FICTION SERIES, $16.95 each

MS-7 **MASTERS OF SCIENCE FICTION AND FANTASY, Vol. Seven**
Lester del Rey, "The Band Played On" and other tales

MS-8 **MASTERS OF SCIENCE FICTION, Vol. Eight**
Milton Lesser, "'A' as in Android" and other tales

If you've enjoyed this book, you will not want to miss these terrific titles…

ARMCHAIR SCI-FI & HORROR DOUBLE NOVELS, $12.95 each

D-91   **THE TIME TRAP** by Henry Kuttner
              THE LUNAR LICHEN by Hal Clement

D-92   **SARGASSO OF LOST STARSHIPS** by Poul Anderson
              THE ICE QUEEN by Don Wilcox

D-93   **THE PRINCE OF SPACE** by Jack Williamson
              POWER by Harl Vincent

D-94   **PLANET OF NO RETURN** by Howard Browne
              THE ANNIHILATOR COMES by Ed Earl Repp

D-95   **THE SINISTER INVASION** by Edmond Hamilton
              OPERATION TERROR by Murray Leinster

D-96   **TRANSIENT** by Ward Moore
              THE WORLD-MOVER by George O. Smith

D-97   **FORTY DAYS HAS SEPTEMBER** by Milton Lesser
              THE DEVIL'S PLANET by David Wright O'Brien

D-98   **THE CYBERENE** by Rog Phillips
              BADGE OF INFAMY by Lester del Rey

D-99   **THE JUSTICE OF MARTIN BRAND** by Raymond A. Palmer
              BRING BACK MY BRAIN by Dwight V. Swain

D-100 **WIDE-OPEN PLANET** by L. Sprague de Camp
              AND THEN THE TOWN TOOK OFF by Richard Wilson

ARMCHAIR SCIENCE FICTION CLASSICS, $12.95 each

C-31   **THE GOLDEN GUARDSMEN**
              by S. J. Byrne

C-32   **ONE AGAINST THE MOON**
              by Donald A. Wollheim

C-33   **HIDDEN CITY**
              by Chester S. Geier

ARMCHAIR SCIENCE FICTION & HORROR GEMS SERIES, $12.95 each

G-9   **SCIENCE FICTION GEMS, Vol. Five**
              Clifford D. Simak and others

G-10   **HORROR GEMS, Vol. Five**
              E. Hoffman Price and others

A LOST WORLD, HIDDEN BENEATH THE ICE

When Jim McClurg signed on to be ship's artist on the Aurora, he thought he was embarking on a long rescue mission, a lengthy sea voyage into ice-infected Arctic waters in search of a lost fur trader, missing some five years. And all he had to do was paint lovely pictures for his eccentric employer. However, the Lady Lucille Lorruth wanted more than to find her missing husband. Somewhere in these frozen wastes was a fortune in furs, left in a secret cache several years earlier. A fortune she coveted perhaps even more than the life of her husband. But guarding them was a strange, beautiful girl—a girl who rode a fantastic white tiger with intelligence and seemingly super scientific powers. Together they guarded the entrance to a fantastic lost world hidden beneath vast layers of glacial ice.

CAST OF CHARACTERS

JIM McCLURG
This starving artist had a unique opportunity—to paint pictures on a long sea voyage into the Arctic for a rich, eccentric woman.

VEEVA
She was young, beautiful, rode the back of a white tiger, and was over twenty thousand years old!

LADY LUCILLE LORRUTH
It was her party—a daring voyage into Arctic waters to find her long, lost husband. But was this her real motive?

STEVE POUND
Second in command, he had to sometimes tiptoe between the whims of a rich, temperamental woman and a drunken captain.

GANDL
This stowaway with a mysterious accent eventually garnered favor from the ship's crew—but who was he really?

CAPTAIN FRENCH
An old drunk with rank and privilege—and a fortune in wealth that was coveted by the woman who employed him.

PROFESSOR PETERSON
One of the only voices of reason on the entire expedition. His knowledge of far-off lands and customs proved to be invaluable.

THE ICE QUEEN

By
DON WILCOX

ARMCHAIR FICTION
PO Box 4369, Medford, Oregon 97504

For more information about Armchair Books and products, visit our
website at…

www.armchairfiction.com

Or email us at…

armchairfiction@yahoo.com

CHAPTER ONE
White Apparition

IF I could only paint this story, instead of writing it, I wouldn't have any trouble getting started. I'd paint a wide green sea full of white icebergs. That would be Baffin Bay. A strip of Greenland coast would show along the right side of the picture, mostly white but with a few patches of bright green verdure. In the center of the picture would be our old two-masted brig, *Aurora*, skimming along gracefully in a northerly direction through a clear channel.

Those two prominent fur-clad figures at the rail, gazing at the coastline through pocket telescopes, would be Lady Lucille Lorruth and Captain French, searching for signs of the Lady's long-lost husband, Lord Lorruth, and his party of fur traders, who entered this wilderness of ice five years ago and failed to return.

The face of Lady Lucille would be reddened with cold; the face of Captain French, dark with whiskers and purplish from too much drink.

A tinge of pink would show in every surface that faced the right of the picture, for the sun of the arctic summer would be somewhere off to the east, skimming low over the mountainous Greenland coast.

I painted many such pictures during the early weeks of our expedition, before the outdoor temperatures went below zero to stay. I was Lady Lucille's official artist and I relished my work. This would be a lark, and a rare opportunity. And when I returned I would be able to give illustrated lecture tours.

My first surprise was my acquaintance with Lady Lucille. It is one thing to know a famous person by reputation, but quite another to develop an intimate friendship of the sort that must exist on board ship. Lady Lucille Lorruth was exceedingly friendly to me. She had the highest praise for my simplest sketches. With childlike exuberance she went about the deck displaying these works to Captain French and Steve Pound, the mate, and any of the crewmembers that happened along.

"Our journey is bound to be successful," she would say, "because we have such a wonderful artist."

"Very, very excellent," Captain French would comment with a big hearty laugh. He was quick to share any interest or enthusiasm of Lady Lucille Lorruth.

Soon I found myself more or less subject to the whims of this vivacious lady who headed our expedition. Though I may have spent a full day at work over the drawing board, I would quickly comply if she suggested another sketch or two to be added to my day's output. Perhaps it was our first glimpse of the northern lights. Perhaps it was a patchwork carpet of ice floes sliding along, forming fantastic designs.

During those early weeks Lady Lucille's slightest wish, I may say, was my greatest pleasure. But I had not yet been fully disillusioned as to the true character of Lady Lucille Lorruth. It took the loss of a life—the life of Inez, the Lady's personal attendant. But that comes later…

ONE day, after we had left the coast of Greenland, I found a picture thumbtacked to my drawing board, which I had not drawn. Shorty Barnes, the comical little deck hand with the saucer eyes, popped in the door after awhile, and I asked him about it.

He blinked. "Didn't you give me strict orders not to destroy no sketches, no matter where I found 'em?"

"This isn't one of my pictures," I said.

"Huh?" He wondered. "Thought it looked like you was slippin' a bit."

"Where'd you find it?"

"Out by the bulwarks driftin' along in the wind."

I stared at the sketch. "I can't even make out what it is. Looks like a woman riding on a horse—or is it a polar bear?"

"Or a four-legged broomstick ridin' a witch, or versa vesuvious," said Shorty. He shrugged and walked away.

Somehow this illustration, crude though it was, must mean something. That was the thought, which kept turning over in my mind. I am enough of an artist to know that people don't draw things without a reason. Even when the schoolboy sketches faces in the sand with his bare toes he is trying to express something, whether he knows it or not.

That night I feel asleep listening to the irregular bump, bump, bump of the loose ice against the hull of the ship. Our easy sailing might come to an end sooner than we expected.

The next day I thumbtacked the sketch near the door of the mess room, knowing that everyone on board would see it at some time or another. Then I watched through the noon hour.

Shorty spied it and he pranced around on his bandy bowlegs, lecturing to a crowd of half a dozen sailors about it. He said it was a mystery. Someone must be trying to run competition to the official artist.

"Jim McClurg said it wasn't his work," said Shorty.

The sailors didn't argue that point. They reckoned that when I painted a four-legged object you could tell whether it was meant for a hippopotamus or a sawhorse. And if I painted a girl you'd know it was a girl, not a witch or a mermaid.

One of the fellows thought he might touch the picture up a bit if someone would lend him a pencil. But just then the three burliest, toughest sailors, the Frabbel brothers, came thudding down the deck.

The Frabbels pushed the rest of the crowd away so they could see. The sketch interested them only slightly. They dismissed it with a few obscene remarks and followed the other sailors into the mess room.

AN HOUR later I noticed that the sketch caught the attention of Lady Lucille. She was being escorted to the Captain's private dining room for her customary early afternoon dinner. On one side of her was the roly-poly purple-faced captain, on the other was her thin, nervous, red-eyed, thirty-five year old maid, Inez.

Of the three, Lady Lucille was as capable as any of walking the decks unsupported, for her maid was too frail to withstand a strong wind, and the captain had already begun his day's drinking. But it was a matter of daily ceremony for the two of them to parade her to dinner. It was Captain French's daily opportunity to remind us that he was a person of great wealth and importance; it was Inez Dorster's ritual of obeisance to nobility.

The picture caught Lady Lucille's attention. But half a glance caused her to turn her head haughtily. Her shoulders swayed stiffly through her fur coat as she quickened her pace past the mess room door.

"What was that?" the captain grumbled, craning back at the picture. "Something to be removed," Lady Lucille snapped. "Not now. Take me to dinner."

She stomped away in angry dignity, as if she was a queen who had been insulted from the streets.

There was no good reason that she should have mistaken the picture for something indecent, although, as I have noted, it was difficult to interpret. But here was a fair sample of Lady Lucille's behavior—her anxiety to demonstrate that she was a much loftier person than the common mortals around her. She world go far out of her way to exhibit delicacies of taste or temperament. And if she became angry over some trifle, everything would come to a standstill. The captain would have to clamp down on the sailors' normal harsh talk and profanity from one end of the ship to the other because Lady Lucille was upset. At such times no one dared to indulge in any cursing except Lady Lucille herself.

The sketch hung on the door for half the afternoon. From my drawing board by the deck rail I could watch it. Cedric Peterson, the geographer, ("Professor" as the sailors called him) strolled along with an open book in his hands. He raised one of his bristling black eyebrows a trifle, but sauntered on, uninterrupted in his reading.

Malonski, the bald-headed, big-toothed steward, limped past with a tray of food for the stowaway, who had been imprisoned below soon after his presence had been discovered.

Late that afternoon Steve Pound came trotting by, just off duty. The picture arrested him instantly. He jerked out the thumbtack, pocketed the paper, and walked off.

I knew, then, that Steve had drawn it.

CHAPTER TWO
A Girl on a Tiger

STEVE POUND was a hard worker and a square shooter—as honest and as straightforward as any man on ship. He would take over an extra work shift for a sick sailor quicker than anyone. He was not one to waste his time dabbling with hobbies, and I couldn't conceive of his having acquired a sudden interest in art.

Well, my curiosity got the best of me and I went to Steve.

"How did you happen to draw it?" I asked him.

"So you were the one who found it," he said. "Come into my room so we can talk."

He closed the door back of us. I noticed the mysterious look in his eyes—a strange glint that contrasted with the usual clear-eyed, square-jawed confidence of his countenance. Steve had spent most of his thirty years on the ocean. He was a solid conservative seaman.

He didn't doubt that these newfangled ships called steamboats might be useful in due time. But he had never stepped aboard a steamboat and he doubted that he ever would. He'd heard all the arguments; but he had heard arguments, too, that some day boats would fly through the air—and that was more than he could believe. Like most of us, living in the middle eighteen hundreds, he knew when he had something solid—and that something was ocean navigation in the traditional manner.

Would he ever leave the sea? Perhaps some day, long enough to build a little cottage on the Newfoundland coast, and find a wife to keep it for him, so that he would have a home between voyages and for his old age.

Steve unfolded the paper and gazed at the sketch.

"You won't believe me, Jim," he said, "but I can trust you. I am going to tell you exactly what I saw that night as we pulled away from the shore of Greenland."

"If you saw it I'll believe it," I said.

"Do you remember that wide glacier? It ended in a cliff of ice along the shore line that paralleled our course for four and a half hours."

"I saw the first hour of it," I recollected, "before I turned in."

"That's where I saw it—this strange, unbelievable thing. Maybe you remember I was late coming off my watch that night. I held on because I kept seeing it."

"What?" I was becoming exasperated.

"I thought at first it was someone riding a polar bear—the hugest bear I'd ever seen. But it wasn't. It was a tiger."

"Tiger?"

"A *white* tiger!" Steve Pound was looking at me steadily. He was in deadly earnest. "If it had happened only once I wouldn't have believed it myself."

"I should think not."

"But I'm not a man to see apparitions, and when I saw it the second time, and caught a clear view of the rider, I knew my eyes weren't fooling me."

"With a rider?" I gasped. "What *are* you talking about?"

"I said you wouldn't believe me but I'm telling you just what I saw. The rider was a girl. I caught a full view of her, riding past the rising moon. She was dressed like something out of a show or a circus—"

I INTERRUPTED to doubt whether Steve Pound had ever seen a circus. But he was too intent on this imaginary image to be bothered.

"Something like a girl I saw in a pageant, one time, up in Norway. She had gold sandals and a skirt of red fox furs and gold breastplates and a helmet with gold wings—"

"You've been dreaming."

"And there was a flashy red robe that fluttered back from her shoulders, and she was pretty—awful pretty. If I had all the words in all the books I couldn't tell you how pretty. I mean it, Jim. I—"

"You saw all this through your telescope?"

"I did. She rode right along the dangerous edge of the glacier, and that white tiger of hers would leap the gaps like a bird."

"Did it have teeth? What color were its eyes? Did you count the whiskers?"

Steve's cheeks flushed with anger.

"Don't get mad," I said. "But you've just had a bad dream——"

"It wasn't bad."

"And you've let it work on your imagination. We were a safe half mile from that ledge of ice when I saw it."

"We edged closer," said Steve. "We were sailing steady and I took a chance, so I could get a better view. I steered within thirty yards. With the telescope I could see the snowflakes fly back from that tiger's feet, all colored against the northern lights."

"It's a wonder you didn't crash us. Was anyone with you?"

"Not a soul. The elder Frabbel had played off his watch. The whole blooming show was all mine."

"I'm sure of it," I said.

Steve Pound stopped, the reason being that he doubted whether there was any use going on. And he was right, because I was fully convinced he was having delusions.

I wanted to walk out and call the ship's physician. But Steve Pound ordered me to sit down.

"We haven't finished," he said. "Not till you give me your opinion. Do you think the girl was following us? Often she seemed to be riding like the wind right toward our ship, especially whenever we drifted straight toward a point. What do you make of it, Jim?"

"I don't know," I said. "I don't know anything about it."

"I've a hunch she wanted to come aboard," said Steve. "Maybe she had a message for us."

For a long time I sat in silence. Finally I said, "*White* tiger? Who ever heard of a white tiger?"

"I've been wondering about that," said Steve earnestly. "Is there such a thing as a polar tiger?"

"No."

"Or a lion—or a panther—or a leopard?"

"Of course not."

"I wish I had called you," said Steve. "No one knows much about this Far North. We're going to see some strange things and it'll take an artist like you, Jim McClurg, to capture them. I tried when I made that sketch, but I can't draw. And besides, when I tried to put it down in a picture, the whole thing began to seem so impossible—"

"It *is* impossible, Steve."

"All right, Jim, you'll see for yourself," Steve said hotly. "We aren't making any more knots than that girl and her tiger. If she comes our way again, I'll call you. If she doesn't—you can forget it."

Exactly one week later the apparition returned and I saw it for myself.

CHAPTER THREE
Suicide

BEFORE I can record the substance of our meeting with that strange pair, the girl and the tiger who were shadowing our ship, I must go back to note a few items about Captain French's wealth and Lady Lorruth's ambitions, the secret terrors of Inez the maid, and the sullen silence of the stowaway we had picked up.

I still don't know at what port the stowaway boarded our ship, but sometime during those two weeks of skirting the Greenland coast we were surprised to find him hiding among the barrels in the hold.

The cook, Malonski, and Steve Pound, the mate, dragged him out on deck and we all got a look at him. He was tall and gaunt, and young—twenty-five at the most—rather too young to be a habitual tramp and vagabond. His ragged overcoat might have been rescued from an incinerator. His hair was very black, and very grimy. But his face showed no lack of spirit. I don't think I ever saw so much fire in the eyes of any man.

"Call the Captain," said Steve Pound, "and Lady Lorruth, too."

The whole crew gathered around staring at this rebellious looking human. From his sullen glare he must have thought we were going to kill him.

We backed away to make room for the captain who escorted Lady Lorruth into the stowaway's presence The captain started blustering, but the real authority was Lady Lucille Lorruth. This was her ship, and her expedition. The pompous captain was more decorative than useful; his reputation as a wealthy bachelor merchant had lent a certain prestige to this rescue party. But Lady Lucille did most of the whip cracking.

It wasn't hard to guess her attitude toward the stowaway from the start. This unkempt stranger was an intruder. He had no business here. Our food stores were limited. He came aboard to thieve a passage, or food, or both.

"Who are you?" Lady Lorruth asked.

In slow heavy words the ragged fellow replied, "My name in Gandl."

"Gandl?" Lady Lorruth's attractive face twisted with suspicion. In her angry moments the narrow stripe of white hair, which crowned her blue-black carefully groomed tresses, seemed to emphasize the blaze of white in her narrow eyes. Her fury was an artist's study: thin flaring nostrils, lips that tightened over her teeth with a hint of brutality. She relished this situation, I think, because it gave her an opportunity to play her ugly authority, causing the most innocent sailor in her audience to quail with feelings of guilt.

"Gandl..." she repeated. "I'll have the captain set you adrift on an iceberg, Gandl, as soon as it suits my pleasure. Straighten up... I said, straighten up!"

The stowaway was already standing as straight as a ruler, though his miserable clothes gave him an aspect of sagging. Lady Lucille's command failed to move him. The captain jumped to his chance, throwing a heavy fist to the stowaway's jaw, knocking him off his feet.

"Get up..." Lady Lucille quietly snarled. "On your feet! There, now stand *straight.*"

The stowaway rose slowly and adjusted his clothes. His expression remained the same—silent, fiery defiance. But Lady Lucille decided that his obedience had improved. She shot a few more questions at him.

"Where did you come from?"

"Back there."

"Where? Greenland—Labrador—Newfoundland?"

"I don't know. It was a long way back." His voice was thick with an accent that was new to me.

"What are you doing here?"

"I'll help you sail through the ice."

LADY LORRUTH glanced at the captain, then at the crew. She tossed her head arrogantly. "We don't need your help. We'll take care of you when the time comes. Captain French, make him fast with chains."

It was several days, then, before Gandl came out of the hold.

We had a week of dodging an ice pack that was bearing down upon us from the north. Daily it grew thicker. We fought to take advantage of every open channel. If we had had a steamboat, even a small tug, it would have been easy. But our brig was equipped only with sails and so we were being tossed about at the caprice of nature.

That was the week that we followed close along the shores of Greenland—the week that Steve Pound saw the strange pair who were following us, and told me about the picture he had drawn.

And on one of those days came the first tragedy of our expedition—the loss of Inez Dorster.

It happened during Lady Lucille's dinner hour.

For some unaccountable reason only the captain had accompanied Lady Lucille to dinner that afternoon. Her maid had been acting strangely, carrying on with much muffled crying and always looking sick from worry. Everyone supposed she was scared over the approaching dangers from the ice. It was bumping the sides of the ship almost constantly. The prospect of being ice-bound through a long arctic winter was a gloomy one for all of us.

Inez Dorster went overboard at two-ten in the afternoon.

Malonski, the cook, saw her fall past his window. He began to shout in Polish, and he fell over a table and a chair on his way to the alarm bell.

For two or three minutes no one could make out what had happened.

Malonski finally made two of the Frabbel brothers understand, and in his eagerness to drive them to the rescue—since he himself couldn't swim—he pushed one of them overboard.

By that time a dozen or more of us had rushed up to see what all the noise was about. The captain missed the whole event, being preoccupied with food and, especially, drink. But Steve Pound, who was supposed to be sleeping, arrived on the scene in time to help rescue Rake Frabbel from his icy plunge.

As to Inez Dorster, she was back there somewhere but we couldn't see her. We were all too late. We circled back, and Steve and Shorty let down a dory, and young Frabbel and I went with them.

WE SEARCHED for the body for two hours, but in the end we had to give up. The ice floes were sweeping down thick and fast with the current. It was a constant fight to keep our dory from being smashed to kindling wood. We were half full of water when we caught the hooks and made our way back to the deck of the *Aurora*.

The captain asked Professor Peterson to read a passage from the Bible and make a prayer, as a sort of funeral service. We were all pretty solemn with the shock of the thing, and especially sorry for Lady Lucille, who looked as if she wanted to cry but couldn't.

More than anything else we were mystified. A woman who has been a faithful maid for ten or fifteen years doesn't suddenly commit suicide unless the world has turned awfully black—and I couldn't see that it had.

But there was no time to wonder about it. "All hands on deck!" was the cry from the bridge. The ice was closing in on us. For hours to come, every man of us was kept busy with hooks and anchors, fighting off the trap.

"We could use a dozen more hands!" Steve Pound yelled, as he flung his weight against a pole, barely thrusting a floater aside. "We could sure use that stowaway."

The captain made no comment. But a few minutes later he returned to the bow leading the gaunt, dark, half-starved figure of Gandl.

"You said you wanted to help," the captain growled. "All right, well see if you're any good."

Within ten minutes an undercurrent of whispering went over the noisy deck… "That damned stowaway is better than any three men."

It was true. Whenever Shorty and I had a chance to go forward for a new catch with our anchor we'd get a glimpse of Gandl at work.

He was out in front of the ship's prow, leaping from one floater to another, prying and splitting them with an iron bar, breaking the path. He was surer on his feet than any mountain goat, and very, very quick, even for a young man.

I wished that Lady Lucille could have seen him. But she had gone to her room to be alone with her sorrows.

Gandl and Steve Pound were the last two men to quit. But at last there was a grinding reverberation that rumbled through the ship. A massive wedge of ice had slid right under our hull. We were lifted bodily. Then—with a loud clunk—we came to a dead stop.

The ice pack was tight around us. We were three miles from land, but the space was rapidly filling with solid ice, so that the continent seemed to spread right out and claim us.

That night everyone was so dog-tired that extra drinks were served all around. The Frabbel brothers bought some of the extras off their fellow sailors, and got drunk and wanted to fight everyone. They stormed around, yelling and cursing and boasting. Then one of them spied the stowaway and started dragging him out on the deck to give him a beating.

But Steve Pound picked up a crowbar and tamed all three of the quarrelsome Frabbels and put them to sleep for the night and a good share of the next day.

CHAPTER FOUR
News from the Dead

BY THE end of the week we decided that it was useless to try to break our way out. We must wait until the ice broke of its own accord before we could pursue our journey. It was a demoralizing situation.

It took Steve Pound to rally our spirits. He insisted that Captain French put us on a rigorous daily schedule of exercise and amusements.

A part of my daily routine was devoted to doing a portrait of Lady Lucille Lorruth. She decided that she wanted a picture of herself, dressed in sumptuous furs, sitting on deck.

The background of the picture was to be the field of ice that enclosed us. Since the temperature was seldom above freezing and often below zero we could only work about an hour at a stretch.

But these hours were full of conversations—some of them highly confidential. Lady Lucille needed someone to talk with, now, more than ever. She was deep in troubles—I had not guessed how deep.

Those troubles went right into the portrait. Try though I would to soften the picture by retouching it with warm colors, something evil crept into it—hardness of greed and the anxiety of secret ambitions.

I purposely ruined the picture one day so I could start over.

On my second trial I made an effort to keep Lady Lucille in a certain mood that I thought would be appropriate to this work. After all, I reasoned, there must be much in her character that was truly noble. She was risking her life to make this expedition.

Why?

Purely for her love and devotion to her dead husband.

What could be more beautiful than an affection so enduring? Ah—that was the theme that my portrait must capture. My painting would fill this face with longing and hope and infinite loyalty.

"Keep your eyes on the distant mountains," I advised. "Can you imagine what hardships an explorer must endure, crossing that rugged terrain?"

"You mean my husband?"

"I often think of him," I said, painting rapidly as I talked. "What a relief it would be to him and his party if we could find them in time... There is always a chance, you know, that they've survived somehow."

"Did I doubt it?" she replied, rather too curtly.

"It would be miraculous, after five years. But if we should succeed, Lady Lucille, I would always believe it a miracle wrought by your faith—your love—your prayers."

"I never pray," she retorted coldly. Again her eyes were narrow and hard.

I CONTINUED to talk with her in terms of hope. It was difficult; like all the others aboard, I felt certain that we would never find Lord Lorruth alive. But like the rest of the crew, I had supposed that Lady Lucille was firm in her faith; that she had come believing and hoping we would find him alive.

All at once I saw that I was mistaken. She didn't believe any such thing.

"Your husband is a very courageous man," I would say. I would purposely stress the word is, to imply that her husband was still living.

"Yes," Lady Lorruth would reply. "He was one of the bravest gentlemen in England."

Note that I quote her as answering in terms of the past rather than the present. I am sure she was not aware she was doing this. But it happened over and over again.

"My husband was a favorite of all the noblemen," she would say. "He was a personal friend of the King."

See what I was driving at? I was proving to myself that Lady Lorruth knew at heart that her husband must be dead.

I kept her gazing at the mountains, but her conversation would bound away from the subject of her lost husband.

"Those mountains are wealth," she would say, and the avarice of her heart would creep right into her portrait. "There must be hundreds of thousands of dollars worth of furs out there waiting to be claimed. Lord Lorruth must have gathered a fortune for me this time."

If I succeeded in diverting her from a contemplation of furs she might lapse into a theme that seemed to give her much mental torture.

"What will the people back in England say when they learn that my maid committed suicide? How can I explain? What will the gossips whisper—about me?"

There seemed to be a very guilty conscience at work.

But if I failed to enrich my portrait with a mood of tragic devotion, I succeeded in capturing some of this inner turmoil. In my own mind I came to the conclusion that Lady Lorruth was sailing under false pretenses. Why had she come? Not because she believed her husband to be alive. It must be from some other motive.

SINCE we were locked against the upper shore of Greenland, we began making daily expeditions on foot. And luckily so, for we discovered, on the point of a cliff, a landmark.

It was a point that most ships would be forced to pass.

The landmark was a cairn of stones standing twelve feet tall. Our sailors dug into the cairn and there they found a steel box, tied closed with a wire.

Inside the box was a letter addressed, "Lady Lucille Lorruth."

You can imagine the excitement on board our ship while we waited on the deck for Lady Lucille to emerge from her cabin to tell us the news.

I was prepared for her apathetic reaction. When she made an effort to respond to the sailors' curiosity and enthusiasm, her manner was a sham. Her show of hope rang false.

"He passed this way," she said. "I think we shall find him if we keep going. He speaks of—uh—furs. An abundance of them. I will tell you more—later."

The sailors were reverently silent. They seemed to be saying, "Poor Lady Lucille. She still thinks we'll find him alive."

The captain rubbed his whiskers dubiously. "Is the letter dated?"

"It bears a date," said Lady Lucille, "of five years ago. But I have faith that everything will be all right. Yes, we'll push right on, as soon as the ice breaks for us. Meanwhile, you must all keep hoping for the best, and—uh—*praying.*"

Her shallow voice carried thin conviction. But the sailors were touched, and she had made the most of their sympathies.

However, her eye caught mine just as she said "praying" and I saw her cheeks flush with anger. She must have read my distrust.

She turned swiftly, clutched the letter to her breast, and hurried off to her room.

CHAPTER FIVE
White Tiger to the Rescue

THE next day the further news from the letter was revealed to us. A gift was waiting for Lady Lorruth—a gift of furs. It had been hidden, according to the letter, in a cache on the next cliff to the north.

This news gave us a tremendous lift of spirit. It gave us something to work for, something in reach while we were still locked in the ice. Immediately Captain French planned a small expedition which was to proceed on foot to the appointed spot.

When I heard that Shorty Barnes was one of the chosen party I couldn't resist tagging along. Shorty Barnes had won the record of falling down more times than any other man on board. I saw in him possibilities of a series of comic cartoons. He was built on the lines of an apple dumpling, his eyes resembled those of a curious pike, and he was invariably getting himself into trouble. He didn't know it, but I had fifteen or twenty sketches of him in characteristic poses— tumbling over the table, being frightened on a night watch, jerked off his feet by the anchor he tossed at an ice drift, and so on.

I had a hunch that the boys would let Shorty take the risks if any were to be taken, and I was right. When we reached the second cliff our way was blocked by a twenty-foot wall of ice. It was a short cut and if we could scale it, it would save us an hour of trudging around a small bay. However, before it was a five-foot neck of water, like a moat in front of an icy castle.

We threw an ice hook to the top of the twenty-foot ledge and it caught fast.

"All right, Shorty, up the rope you go," said Captain French.

Shorty was game. He went up the rope hand over hand, but just as he reached the top of the twenty-foot ascent a strange thing happened.

The pack of ice cracked and split wide open. It spread about four feet in one sudden vertical break. It was like an explosion. The anchor was left without support. Shorty, rope, and anchor and all went down, smack into the water.

Comedy turned to near tragedy on the spot. Every one of us was dressed in heavy furs. A leap into that icy pool would mean coming to grips with death itself.

Shorty wailed in a blood-chilling tone. But there was hope in that outcry, and in his clumsy struggle—as though he had decided this was a good time to learn to swim.

I supposed Steve Pound would be the first man to the rescue.

But it was our stowaway who plunged. He went in like a seal. You would think he'd lived in icy waters all his life. In a moment he was out again with ice collecting on his bristling black stubble and a deathly white Shorty in his arms.

Now the only thing to do was to send part of our party back with Shorty as swiftly as possible.

NO FURS were found. Nothing was accomplished that would give Lady Lucille any satisfaction.

But what made the greatest impression on all of us was that our stowaway had proved himself, for the second time, a hero.

Lady Lorruth was not impressed. She did not even pretend to be. She had taken an icy dislike to Gandl from the first.

After he had helped so valiantly in our fight with the floe ice, I supposed he would gain her favor. But instead, the relationship had taken a turn for the worse, owing to a very frank and blunt statement of Gandl's—a speech that was frightfully shocking to Lady Lucille's nerves.

It had happened that very morning before we started off to look for the furs. Gandl was no longer in chains. He was sharing Shorty's cabin—an accommodation that he had certainly earned, and that Steve Pound had arranged he should have.

When Lady Lucille announced that there would be a search for the furs, Gandl was on hand to volunteer.

"But we won't find furs," Gandl had asserted in his thick drawling voice. "Five years is too long. They will be gone."

"I have faith in my husband," Lady Lucille snapped in a haughty manner.

"He may be gone too," Gandl said very solemnly. His innocent manner was genuine. He believed that Lady Lucille had not faced this possibility.

Her anger was rising, but she tried to silence him with a sarcastic retort. "You know entirely too much."

"Yes, I do. I know why the other lady chose to die. And you know, too. Because I heard—"

"Hsssh!" Steve Pound warned, and Gandl fell silent.

But Lady Lucille turned a variety of colors and her arms stiffened like vibrating metal.

"It's a lie. It's a lie!" she cried, and she shook her head so violently that the flesh of her cheeks and throat became a shapeless shuddering. As the captain hastily led her away we could all hear her mutter under her breath, "I can't stand that man. I can't stand him…"

But in spite of Lady Lucille, Gandl was a valuable addition to our crew. Twice in the presence of danger he had proved himself a man of phenomenal ability.

THE very next day there were signs that the ice was about to break up and set us free. At noon Lady Lorruth called the stowaway for a conference. And the whisper went around the ship that she had changed her attitude toward him.

Steve and I were present, and I must admit that she was doing her best to seem friendly to the slow, bewildered, ragged young man.

"Gandl, they tell me you helped bring Shorty Barnes back?" she said.

"Yes."

"Then you didn't help the men search for the furs?"

"No."

"They tell me that you were very confident at climbing over the ice," she said.

"Thank you, your ladyship."

"I'll send you back," said Lady Lorruth. "You will go by yourself. Where the others failed, you may succeed. I want you to go and look for the hidden furs."

"After five years, I do not think—"

"Never mind what you think. You are to start at once, and look thoroughly."

"I shall start at once," said Gandl with a respectful bow.

And he did. Within an hour he disappeared from sight over the hummock ice. And that was when Lady Lorruth again took personal command of the ship.

"Captain French, I want you to get us out of here at once. Get the whole crew to work. Use the dynamite if necessary. Get us into that channel. Anything, just so we break free."

The captain looked puzzled.

"We are getting free," he said dubiously. "Within an hour—"

"We have not an hour to waste. Not even a minute. We must go now."

"But what about Gandl? You sent him on an errand. If you think he'll find a cache of furs—"

"Didn't you tell me you found the cache empty?" said Lady Lucille.

"Yes, but what if Gandl—"

"Don't ask stupid questions. Hurry."

We worked like beavers, every one of us, chopping and dynamiting, risking our lives to force a path through the ice.

After three hours we were free. We broke into a long crooked channel with ice floes grinding and scraping on all sides.

The channels widened. The gales pushed us along northward. We were almost out in the open.

"What about Gandl?" Shorty shouted. "He's still over there somewhere. Aren't we going to wait for Gandl?"

None of us knew what to say. This looked like deliberate murder. Out of the corners of our eyes we watched Lady Lorruth. Her lips tightened brutally.

Shorty began to pounce around the deck trying to attract someone's attention. "Gandl! Gandl! What about him? He'll get left. What's the idea—"

Shorty's wail was cut short suddenly. The captain biffed him across the head, and Shorty went toppling down against the rail.

That was a moment of sullen silence for all of us. It was a true test of the captain and Lady Lorruth. All of us saw their true colors now.

NO ONE said very much. No one dared. Shorty Barnes got up and started limping around the deck. His eyes were deep with hurt and resentment. We were watching him. He walked into the bow, stood there for a long time staring out into the deep.

Many of the crew was still murmuring over what had happened when they noticed that Shorty was pointing. There was a narrow passage ahead. A peninsula from the island where the furs were supposed to be hidden jutted out about half a mile and threatened to block our path. A channel left between it and a field of pack ice looked to be no more than thirty yards wide. The danger in that narrow pass was crowding down on us.

The gale had stiffened. We were making five or six knots. If we could clear the pass, all was well. But for all we knew there might be a floor of ice just up ahead, out of immediate sight.

Steve Pound studied the current through his pocket telescope. The captain shouted orders to everyone.

But what Shorty Barnes was pointing at was neither the narrow pass nor the current but something far more breathtaking.

He began to mumble, "What is that thing? Come here. Come here, George. Do you see what I see?"

George and Bill and a whole cluster of crewmen saw. It might have been a statue in ice. It might have been the largest polar bear that we ever encountered. At the distance of one hundred and fifty yards we could not yet be sure that it was anything alive—only that it was something shaped like a massive white animal.

Steve Pound edged close to me.

"All right, Jim, get your sketch pad. That's what I told you about the other day."

I obeyed—reluctantly. But by the time I began drawing I knew what I was sketching—not some ice imitation, but a real live *polar tiger.*

The big beast crept slowly toward the water's edge.

Some of the sailors had gone for firearms. For once neither the captain nor Lady Lorruth had the presence of mind to give any orders.

Suddenly the animal turned and bounded up over the icy bank and disappeared.

A moment later it reappeared at the top of the ledge. Now it bore a rider.

How in the name of heaven it was possible for these two creatures to be inhabiting the waste of ice was more than anyone could guess. But we all saw. We couldn't deny our eyes. And it was the most breathtaking sight I've ever looked upon—that beautiful white tiger was being ridden by a breathtakingly beautiful girl...

I dropped my sketchpad. The men forgot about their guns. We were like statues of ice, then, gazing out at the amazing sight.

The girl rode southward along the mountainous peninsula, and we crowded astern to watch her.

Suddenly she bounded out of sight, then she reappeared around a bulwark of hummock ice.

At last she stopped, some five hundred yards to our rear. She reached down to help someone else onto the tiger. It was our stowaway, Gandl. She came racing back with him.

BUT this time our ship was nosing straight into the narrow channel and a swift current was bearing us forward. In our confusion we entrusted ourselves to Steve Pound. It was up to him to steer us through this perilous pass. But we were too much hypnotized to watch him. All eyes were on the tiger's race to meet us.

It was a race. The girl was speeding back to us, bringing Gandl. Just as we passed through the narrows, that strange white tiger bounded over the last hill of ice and tore down the bank in a flurry of flying snow.

The beast stopped short of the water's edge. The girl clung to its furry neck. Her other arm released Gandl. He bounded down, raced across the last few steps of the icy shore slipped into the water, clothes and all. A moment later he climbed up the ladder and was safely aboard.

But we were no longer paying any attention to Gandl. Rather we were drinking in the picture before us—our nearest view of the tiger and its rider retreating along the promontory of ice.

I tried to catch the details of color and costume. Already the girl and her mount had turned to race away.

As Steve Pound had said, she was like something out of a Viking storybook. Her gold helmet was adorned with wings. She was wearing jeweled breastplates. She was bearing a gold sword. Her wrists were ornamented with bracelets and I was aware that there was a tinkling of bells in rhythm with the movement of her arms. There seemed to be something familiar in this ring, but at the moment I couldn't catch what is was.

The girl was certainly not dressed for arctic weather. The flowing red robe fluttered back from her shoulders loosely. The beautiful skirt of red fox fur was much too short to protect her bare knees.

But all in all it was as bright and gay a costume as one could hope to see in a circus.

It gave me the feeling that the whole spectacle—girl, tiger, costume and all, must have somehow escaped from the world's finest trained animal show—or was this snow-covered country a land of ghosts?

Lady Lucille's outcry broke our gasping silence. Pointing at the girl's costume, she shrieked, "My furs! They're mine— I know it! *My furs...my furs!*"

CHAPTER SIX
The Captain Confides

WE WERE a deckful of question marks. Nobody could make sense out of what had just happened. The girl had ridden completely out of sight. Only the foot tracks convinced us that what we had seen was real.

But here was Gandl. We couldn't doubt him.

At that moment Gandl was glaring daggers at Lady Lucille. Every one of us guessed how he felt. For all we knew, he may have believed that all of us had tried to give him the slip. But no one offered him any explanation.

Lady Lorruth continued to stare at the bank of ice where the rider had disappeared.

Suddenly she turned on Gandl. Instead of making excuses for her treachery, she faced him accusingly.

"Who was that woman?" she demanded. "Where did she come from? Why did she bring you back here?"

Gandl's silence was defiant.

Lady Lucille's eyes blazed. "Those furs she had—they were mine. I know they were. Lord Lorruth described them in his letter. Who is she? Why did she dare—"

"To bring me back?" Gandl said quietly. "Perhaps so you could send me on another errand."

His voice was deep with suppressed emotion. The situation was charged with an electricity of quiet intenseness. It was something that we all felt. If I had been drawing it in a caricature, Lady Lorruth would have had a knife behind her back and Gandl would have had his fists clenched, hanging at his sides.

So perfect was his control, though, that he simply stood motionless. His drenched clothes were turning to ice.

"Don't talk to him now," said Captain French. "Give him a chance to change before he freezes to death."

"But I insist that he tell me—"

"Later," the captain growled. "We'll have him talking in due time."

The captain flipped a hand at Steve, who understood. He and Shorty led Gandl into a room to help him into warm clothing.

"Back to your work, the rest of you," the captain ordered.

I went back to my drawing board but did no work. Out of the window I could see small blocks of ice passing us; after the echoes of particularly violent cursing on the part of the Frabbel brothers I would see a sizable bit of iceberg float by, dangerously close. But we were safely through the narrows, and it might be expected that our normal routine would soon return.

Captain French, not one to enjoy the many details of his own job, never missed a chance to turn work over to Steve Pound.

The first thing I heard, on awaking from a long night's sleep, was the captain's voice.

"Mr. Pound, I'm giving you the responsibility of questioning Gandl."

"Gladly" said Steve.

"Find out all you can. Lady Lucille is quite upset. Couldn't eat her food last night. Swore she wouldn't sleep till she learned who that 'tiger woman' was. She figures the furs were hers, and there might even be hundreds more like them."

"I'll see what I can learn."

A LITTLE later Steve Pound rapped at my door. I invited him in and closed the door after him. He began casually.

"Well, Jim, you saw?"

"Of course."

"And you're convinced?"

"I was never more mystified in my life. What does it mean, Steve?"

"I haven't had a talk with Gandl yet," said Steve. He lighted a pipe. "We won't get anywhere playing enemies with him. But he's well placed in Shorty's room. Shorty won't stand for it if anyone tries to harm him. He's a god to Shorty."

"And rightly so," I said, "considering how he can climb over ice, and considering that Shorty had his life saved by him. Did the captain want to chain Gandl up?"

"I talked him out of it," said Steve. "I figure that if we give the fellow decent treatment he'll come through with the information we want. Don't you think so, Jim?"

"Maybe. He doesn't talk much. Somehow I have a feeling he may know plenty, if you could get him to unwind in his own language. Did you ever find out what nationality his name is?"

"It's a funny thing," said Steve. "He didn't know what to say when I asked him whether it was a first name or last name. His only name is Gandl, he said."

Steve gathered up a few of my pencils and some paper and told me to come along. We went back to Shorty's room, listened at the door, heard nothing. Steve knocked.

The door opened. Gandl was smiling. We walked in and closed the door behind us.

For an hour we talked, and I began to catch the drift of Steve's conversation. It was a subtle probe to find out how much Gandl knew of the arctic.

We were on the right trail. When it came to knowledge of seals, polar bears, the life of Eskimos, even the varieties of stunted trees and arctic vegetation, Gandl knew it all. Often he lacked the words to express his ideas, but our pencil sketches helped.

"How far do you want to go with us?" Steve finally asked.

Gandl, still smiling, answered, "As far north as you go."

Steve nodded. "I think it will be all right. Don't be frightened by the Captain or Lady Lucille. We want to be your friends, Gandl. Jim, here, is your friend. So is Shorty. And there's Professor Peterson—he's a square fellow. Let us know if you ever feel like talking with someone."

With that we went out.

DOWN the deck we met the captain, pacing back and forth in great agitation.

"Well, what did you find out? Did he open up?"

"Not much today," said Steve. "There'll be more later."

The captain muttered under his breath.

"I told you to get those answers. Lady Lucille is threatening to have a nervous breakdown. She wants us to find out about the furs and I swear she'll have us torture that damned stowaway with hot irons if we don't get the information she wants soon."

"You'd never find out anything that way," said Steve. "You leave it to me. There'll be plenty of days before we reach our destination."

"What makes you so sure we've got any destination?" said the captain sarcastically. "Lady Lucille can change her plans overnight if she's a-mind to. We may be headed south tomorrow."

"We won't be," said Steve. His manner was sharp and I suddenly realized that he was playing a trump that he had held back. He pointed out to the vast line of snow-covered mountains. "There are too many valuable furs out there for us to turn back, Captain. You know Lord Lorruth's success as well as I. He didn't come up here prepared to spend three years for nothing."

"What do you mean?" said the captain.

"I mean that there are probably a few million dollars' worth of furs stored in some cache. Lady Lucille knows it. So do you. We're not a rescue party. What we've come after is those furs."

The captain's lips drew back tight and cold. His eyes would not meet Steve's or mine. He looked out across the land as if lost in thought. Finally he said, "If Lord Lorruth left furs, Lady Lucille deserves to have them."

"I agree with you completely," said Steve. "If Lady Lucille had just admitted it, instead of pretending, she might have saved herself some trouble."

"Are you thinking of that suicide?" the captain blurted.

"What made you think of that?" Steve asked.

"That damned stowaway has been talking too much," Captain French grumbled.

"He hasn't said any more about it," Steve declared. "But I figure Inez Dorster was pretty badly disillusioned."

The captain shrugged off this matter as a minor irritation. He returned to the subject of furs.

"I'll talk with her right away," he said. "Maybe she'll see the sense of going on."

"I'm sure of it," said Steve. "What's more, she knows as well as the rest of us that we'll never find Lord Lorruth alive."

It was difficult to tell how the captain was going to take these challenging statements from his mate. He stomped up and down the deck a few times before he said anything more. Then he came back and offered his hand to Steve.

"Well," the captain said, "I'm glad we've got this straight. Now I can say a few things to you in confidence. They've been on my mind for quite a while, and now I can tell them to you."

"And to Jim, too?" Steve asked, trying to make sure I got in on it.

"Of course," the captain smiled big-heartedly. "I've confided with Jim from the first. But this particular secret— well, I haven't confided it to anyone until now. Boys, I'm the happiest man on the whole wide ocean. I'm planning to marry Lady Lucille."

I responded with a half-choked, "Huh?"

"I figure it's the best thing for her," said the captain magnanimously, "seeing as how she's been so upset over realizing her husband must be gone for good. So one of these days when the ice closes in on us again we'll get out the weddin' bells."

CHAPTER SEVEN
Slippery Slide

I SHOULD mention that our geographer, Cedric Peterson, was an earnest old "professor" who carried the only supply of books on board. There was one dingy little volume bound in black and white stripes entitled, *The Great Maledictions of History.*

The little book had passed from one to another of us. Considerable controversy had grown out of it, and considerable fun.

Out of courtesy we turned our most interesting reading matter over to Lady Lorruth. She had kept this particular volume for several weeks.

Now a new whispered rumor made the rounds: Lady Lucille was getting a hunch that our expedition was under some kind of a curse.

I didn't know whether there was any foundation for this rumor. But I did know that Lady Lucille was afflicted by a few common superstitions; and now that a general state of bewilderment and confusion had seized all of us, it was natural that she should grasp at straws of magic and sorcery.

As a matter of fact, our very conditions of privation and isolation made it difficult for any of us to keep our balance.

We would overemphasize trifles. We would quarrel over slight privileges, and if the Frabbel brothers were in on it the quarrels would turn into fights. Enmities would flare up, sudden and intense.

Or on the other hand, friendships would become magnified—perhaps all out of proportion to their value.

At any rate, all of us were a little less confident of ourselves and our knowledge and our reasoning powers after our shocking contact with the impossible—the girl and her tiger.

"Maybe Lady Lucille is right," some of the sailors said. "Maybe there is a curse on this ship."

And so the ideas set forth in the little volume of "Great Maledictions" began to spread among us to be taken seriously and to do damage.

When discussions grew serious I discovered that many of the sailors believed there were such things as spiritual curses. All of us became exceptionally sensitive to every troublesome event that occurred.

"Have you noticed," Steve said to me one day, "that Lady Lucille has quit asking about the girl and the white tiger? At first she wanted to know whether Gandl knew anything. But now her mind is settled."

"What's her answer?"

"She's decided the girl and the tiger are impersonating an evil spirit."

"Why *evil?*" I asked.

"You know Lady Lucille as well as I do," said Steve. "That girl was terribly beautiful. What woman could help feeling an instinctive jealousy? But the important thing is that matter of lost furs. If they're not found, Lady Lucille's suspicions will conjure up curses for a long time to come."

"Did you ever see her letter from Lord Lorruth?" I asked.

"No. In fact, I think she destroyed it. But she claims there was a map describing his regular hunting circuit and locating the caches when he was storing the furs."

"We should do some exploring as soon as possible. If we could find one rich cache she might be willing to turn back. There's too much trouble gathering, Steve. It isn't healthy. If I'd known what she was like before I signed up—"

"Don't say it, Jim. Look at the bright side. As an artist, what was it worth to you to catch a glimpse of that tiger girl?"

THE very thought gave my spirits a lift.

"What I wouldn't give to see her again."

"You and I," said Steve, "are going to make an expedition to the shore beyond. We're going to find that girl. If Gandl will go with us, all the better. Are you game, Jim?"

"What do you think we can accomplish?"

"I think," said Steve, "that we can find out about Lord Lorruth—when he died, and where. The girl may even know where his body is. What's more, she may be able to lead us to the furs."

I shook my head. "That's a long shot in the dark, Steve."

"But it's worth a try. It's stupid of the captain and Lady Lucille not to make friends, if possible, and play their friendships to an advantage."

"People don't go out making friends with evil spirits."

"Great guns, I hope you're not swallowing all this curse talk. Heaven knows she's a mystery, but I'm damned if I'll doubt that she's a sure-enough living human being. I'd like to talk with her."

"Have you suggested this to the captain?"

"He hasn't been taking kindly to my suggestions," said Steve. "He distrusts me because of my friendship with Gandl. That's why I'm ready to take a chance."

"When do we go?"

Steve looked at the sun lying low along the southern horizon.

"In a few days the winter darkness will be on us. How much warning will you need?"

"An hour."

The hour's warning came late in September. We struck out in the dory. Our ship had lain almost motionless for a week, but the winter's ice hadn't gathered in on us as yet.

A few of our crew had talked of excursions to the mainland to try their luck at hunting bear or seal. Steve had managed to rig up this party as a scouting trip preliminary to a series of bear hunts. On this pretext he limited the group to Gandl, himself, and me.

ON THE shore we crawled along the icy terrain with the aid of ice hooks and ropes until we reached the temporary safety on the top surface of a snow-covered glacier.

Steve had brought his pocket telescope and he kept peering off toward every mountain of ice expectantly.

"She's probably watching us this very minute," he said. "More than a dozen times during the past week I've caught sight of her off here in the distance."

"I can't understand why she should be following us."

Steve couldn't offer any satisfactory explanation. But I knew he had a theory that there was some mysterious connection between the girl and Gandl. That's why he had made it a point to bring Gandl along.

As for Gandl, he trudged along in his customary silence, but he frequently regarded his ragged clothing and seemed a bit uncomfortable over his appearance. That was a good sign.

"It's practically a proof," Steve whispered to me, as our mysterious third partner marched ahead, "that he expects to meet her."

A flurry of snow came sweeping down on us from the left. It flew past us at an almost unbelievable speed. It was them! It was a breathtaking spectacle of fierce beauty—girl and tiger riding like the wind.

In their wake a puff of icy air blasted against our cheeks. I stopped in my tracks, feeling that a stroke of paralysis had got me. Gandl, too, had halted. Only Steve had the presence of mind to beckon and callout a welcome.

"Hello-o-o-o!"

The girl raced her tiger to the top of the mountainous ridge before she stopped. Then she turned and looked down at us. Her beauty was full of boldness and ferocity and the appeal of youth. She laughed, and her rippling voice carried down to us like the an eerie, tantalizing music.

"Hello-o-o-o, up there!" Steve repeated. "Where are you going?"

"I'm not going any place. I live here," the girl called back in an echoing voice. "Where do you think you are going?"

"She speaks English!" I exclaimed. There was a richness about her voice that seemed to fill the whole outdoors. It was a voice that rang with a high spirit that was at once merry and robust and daring; more than that, it contained a mysterious eternal quality—something I couldn't understand.

The girl had the advantage over us in every way. We tried to hurry toward her. But it was all that Steve and I could do to keep our balance and keep moving along this icy surface. It was hard for us to talk against the blasting winter gale. Our lips and cheeks were too nearly frozen.

As for Gandl, he had apparently decided to remain paralyzed.

But the girl was right in her element. Mounted on this remarkable beast, she could cavort about this treacherous landscape without the slightest thought of danger. She could ride into the icy winds like a phantom all the while laughing and shouting.

"Come on up," she cried.

STEVE and I both began looking around for a suitable path, Gandl came to our rescue now, and led us up through the short canyon of ice and rocks, picking his step as cunningly as a mountain goat. We followed him.

Even so, we were likely to take many minutes to the task of ascending. This was much too slow for the girl. With an emphatic gesture she called to us.

"Never mind, I'll come down."

And down she came, bounding at a full gallop.

I'll never forget that sight, of the flying cloud of snow, the beautiful girl laughing, the snow-white tiger's ferocious face growing larger and larger and larger with every jump of the swift approach.

Suddenly my terror of the beast went to my throat. I probably cried out. I don't remember. I know that my blood went frozen.

Gandl shouted, "Flatten!" and he dropped to the ice.

But Steve and I each darted off in different directions. The next thing I knew I had lost my footing and was sliding down a long slippery pathway. I didn't know where it would end. I swerved and spun and kept on sliding.

"Where are you going?" the girl's voice called. I managed to catch a glimpse of her as she leaped off the beast. She had reached the point where a moment before the three of us had stood. Now there was only Gandl to greet her, and he was peering down at me, shouting at me to stop.

What had happened to Steve I could only wonder. He had fallen out of sight on the other side and was still sliding.

The best I could do was to hurl myself clear of the rocks and sharp projections of ice, one after another. My long slide was a rapid-fire exercise in dodging death, for most of the time I was caroming helplessly.

At last I found myself stranded on a heap of glaciated boulders near the ocean's edge. I looked up. No longer could I see any of my original party. As my eyes took in the new scene, the only familiar sight was the brig lying nearly a mile out at sea, and it was fast disappearing in a blanket of opaque mist.

I lay there, rubbing my arms and legs to make sure I was still all-together, and pulled my torn ruffled clothes into shape. I felt pretty angry at myself for my clumsiness. I tried to feel angry toward the girl, too. But that emotion wouldn't work.

Instantly I was determined to clamber back to the top of the ridge. She would be up there. Steve and Gandl would be talking with her.

I tried to get up.

But with a painful groan I dropped back to my bed of ice for a moment's rest.

A few deep breaths; another moment or two of resting... How dark and thick that mist was growing. Surely I wasn't falling asleep... That would be unwise, just now...very unwise...but so very comfortable.

CHAPTER EIGHT
Instantaneous Igloo

I AWOKE to the sound of crunching footsteps.

A polar bear? No, a polar tiger. It came toward me out of the mist, its huge cat-face looming large, its yellow eyes gleaming.

Within a few yards of me the beast stopped.

Back of it was the foggy background of dark water. I was still lying where I had landed at the bottom of the slide.

I seized my revolver, made ready to shoot.

Then a voice spoke a low command.

"Don't pull the trigger. That's Whitey. He brought me down here to pick you up. Please don't shoot him."

I turned to see the girl standing beside me. She bent down and helped me to my feet. Very much ashamed of my fear, I put my gun away.

"Come, Whitey," she called. "He's awake now. We'll take him back."

The beast's big shoulders moved gracefully as he ambled up beside me. The girl helped me on.

It was the strangest ride I ever had, borne along by the swift rhythmic trot of "Whitey." The light hold of the girl's arm around my waist was enough to keep me from slipping off the tiger's back. We ambled up one steep bank after another. In the smoky mist I lost all sense of direction.

My cold-numbed muscles began to feel a returning warmth; and this was puzzling, in view of the freezing temperature. *It was a mellow, restoring warmth that radiated from the body of the polar tiger.*

I bent to press my face against the animal's furry back, to test my discovery. Yes, there was an aura of electric warmth hovering about this beast.

So that was why this girl could survive in these frozen wastes, defying the deadly blizzards.

At last we were back upon the topmost ridge of rocks.

Imagine my delight when I heard voices and looked up to see Gandl and Steve Pound waiting for me.

"Here we are, safe at last, thanks to the young lady," said Steve Pound.

The young lady and Gandl were, at the moment, looking at each other with serious intense expressions. But the girl turned to us and studied us through her merry, curious eyes.

"You men are quite brave to come exploring in this weather. Don't you know a blizzard is due?"

"We'd better get back to the ship," said Steve. "Will you come with us?"

"There wouldn't be time," said the girl. "The storm is about to break."

"We'll have to make camp," Gandl said in his low all-wise manner, and he led the way to a deep little canyon wedged protectively within two jutting arms of mountain.

THIRTY minutes later we were gathered around a blazing campfire. I took in the picture hoping that sometime I could paint it. We were in the semi-darkness of the approaching arctic night. To our right the skies were red and blue with twistings, spiraling streaks—a gorgeous aurora borealis. We could hear the snapping and threshing of electrical activity. It was a scene rife with color from faraway to near at hand; for the crackling fire, too, was a rare mixture of colored flames. Incidentally, I must note that this fire was another proof of Gandl's ingenuity: he had somehow found an abundance of fuel hidden under the icy ledges.

The four of us, then, sat in comparative comfort—three men and this entrancingly beautiful creature out of the Viking storybook. Back at a little distance was the white tiger curled up for a catnap, its eyes half-closed.

All in all, I thought, here was the most exotic picture that I had ever encountered. I must paint this. As long as I live I'll never see anything quite so colorful or romantic.

But there I was wrong. For although I did not know it at the time, this was only my first approach to a new world—a world so completely exotic as to leave all reality in a limbo of the past.

The girl's rippling laughter dominated the mood of our campfire visit. She seemed so very enthusiastic over meeting with strangers—and Steve and I *were* strangers, but I was not so sure about Gandl.

When the girl told us that her name was Veeva, I couldn't help wondering whether she and Gandl might be members of the same racial stock.

Steve and I were eager to talk with her seriously. We bombarded her with dozens of questions. We wanted to know how she got here and where she lived, and how she had managed to follow along with our boat. Where had she gotten that superbly trained beast and how could she manage to find food for herself in all this wilderness of ice.

We had meant to get around to the subject of Lord Lorruth and his hidden furs. But our natural curiosity about Veeva crowded everything else out.

However, we were initially unable to get any hard information from her. She liked to laugh too well and had every advantage over us, so she told us only what pleased her.

"Food for Whitey?" she echoed. "Of course he has to be fed. Whitey is a ravenous eater... Carnivorous? Certainly."

"He eats fish, then?" Steve suggested.

"Only when he has to," said Veeva. "He much prefers human flesh."

I must have shuffled uneasily, for she quickly added, "But he's very well behaved. You three handsome gentlemen needn't have any fears."

Steve began to catch the spirit of her remarks and he winked at me.

"We'd better not let your tiger see Shorty Barnes. He's one of our plumpest crewmen."

"And we'd better look out for the captain," I said. "The captain would be good eating. He's better fed than anyone."

The girl laughed. "Just wait until you get shelved on top of the winter's ice. We'll be over, Whitey and I, and see if you don't have a few persons on board that you don't really need. Whitey will take care of them."

WE TURNED the subject abruptly. "Where did you get that name Veeva?"

"I can't remember that far back," said the girl.

"Is it a Norse name?" I asked.

She shook her head. "It comes from much further back than that—much, *much* further. I really can't remember."

This was a strange statement, and I wanted to believe she was only joking. But again I caught that mysterious impression of something timeless and eternal. Only a delusion, I thought, accentuated by the deep gray mists, and the strange colored light of the fire.

"Gandl tells me that you're a queen," Steve said presently.

I pricked up my ears at this. It was news to me. Steve must have had some conversation with Gandl that I had missed—probably during the interval in which she had come to my rescue.

"I am a queen," Veeva answered simply, and she wasn't laughing.

"Queen?" I gasped, and instantly a blunt question escaped my lips. "Who is the king?"

She looked at me sharply. All at once the merriment was gone from her eyes and in its place was an expression of suppressed hurt. I stumbled to recover myself but probably made matters worse.

"That is—er—if there's a queen then there must be a king—and I just wondered—"

Steve came to my rescue. "What Jim means is, he's jealous because he's not the king. Isn't that it, Jim?"

"How'd you guess it?" I snapped, kicking awkwardly at a burning log. "You must be jealous yourself."

"Maybe I am," said Steve. "Who knows? Maybe I could have been a king if I'd been born in the right family."

"I can say that too," I retorted. "What does a king have that I don't have?"

"A kingdom, for one thing," the girl said.

"And for another," said Gandl, with a low laugh, "a queen."

This talk had gotten a little under Steve's skin as much as mine. He rose impetuously.

"If I were a king," he said, "I'd have the queen—don't worry."

I didn't like it, the way his eyes were staring down at Veeva, with her smiling up at him. I rose up.

"And if *I* were a king—"

But Gandl broke in with, "Maybe you men would like to fight for it." His subtle, yet withering sarcasm made both of us feel foolish. We settled down and stared into the fire.

But the whole conversation had evidently annoyed Veeva's merry mood.

"Such talk..." she said. With an impetuous gesture to her pet tiger she sprang up. The tiger ran to her. She leaped to catch its mane, flung herself to its back and went racing away.

GANDL gave a low disappointed growl.

"Where is she going?" I asked.

Gandl shook his head. "You see, she *is* a queen. She doesn't care for petty arguments."

"We acted a bit foolish," Steve said. Then he bounded up and ran in the wake of the flyaway snow. He cupped his hand and shouted with all his powerful voice.

"*Veeva!* Please come back... *Veeva!*"

I joined him, and the two of us kept calling. Our voices echoed back through the fog.

"*Vee-ee-eeva!*"

Instantly it happened.

Perhaps no scientist has ever lived who has seen that peculiar combination of forces in action. To us it was a magical phenomenon. It happened as we shouted, and for an instant it swallowed up the very echo of our voices.

A sphere of ice formed over us.

It happened like a swift flash of light. At once it cut off the sight of the retreating girl. It blocked out the color of the aurora, thrust away the sight of the sky, the mountains, and every object that was more than forty feet away from us. It enclosed us completely—

"*Veeva!*" Steve shouted, and this time his voice echoed round and round within the sphere of ice as if it were a solid stone cave.

CHAPTER NINE
Frozen Waves

OUR voices softened to whispers. It was a ghastly weird enclosure that we were in and the curves of the ice over our heads flickered with the reflection of the colored firelight.

So perfect was this spherical temple that every breath of sound was magnified over and over. The crackle of fire was like the rapping of thunder traveling around and around until it melted away in the emptiness of the place.

"What caused this?" Steve asked. "Where did it come from?"

"It must have fallen," I suggested, "just like a big nutshell—"

"Over three nuts," Gandl said dryly. He seemed not the least disturbed.

But Steve's eyes were roving back and forth with unspeakable curiosity.

"There's an electric storm up in the sky," said Steve. "There must be electrical winds that have created this ice—somehow."

"How can an electric storm, or any other storm, make such a ceiling of ice," I argued. "It happened *instantly*. We know that much. And it couldn't have dropped down out of a cloud or it would have blown us off our feet. Besides, the whole structure would have smashed to smithereens."

My final word echoed with a weird ring and faded to silence. Now we could hear the sleet and snow beating down upon our magic igloo.

"I think," said Steve, "that the girl must have clamped this icehouse on us. She's full of tricks. She might have drawn a wide net, and it caught the mist—"

I speculated upon this but it didn't seem possible. In fact, the whole happening was so devilishly mystifying that Steve and I were talking without rhyme or reason.

Then Gandl said, "The sound did it. I've seen it happen before."

"Sound? You mean thunder or something?"

"Not thunder. Your own voices calling 'Veeva.' I've seen it happen before."

"Why, that's outlandish," I somewhat growled. "How could we bring on an ice roof just by calling her name?"

"Stop it," Steve warned. "If you bring on another one we might be buried in tons of ice. How thick is that ice, anyhow? Where do we get out?"

WE BROKE through the lower edge of the six-inch crust of ice. For the next hour we trudged around through the swirling sleet and snow, examining this strange icy temple, trying to understand its form.

It was as big as a small church. It had materialized around us like something out of a void. It had imprisoned us just in time to let that beautiful girl who called herself a queen, ride away from us, heedless of our calls.

The small valley in which this spherical prison was located was shaped like an A. And now we noticed that the sphere had locked itself over each of the side arms of this triangular formation. Here was a strange thing. There was no bulge beyond the outer circumference of the sphere at any point. But we remembered that on the inside there had been several small bulges. We returned inside to examine them by the waning firelight.

THE accumulating warmth was causing little rivers of melting ice to creep outward from the zenith, like ribs of a liquid fan, spreading into a huge crystal starfish of icicles. Soon this place would become dangerous with falling ice. But we must examine those bulges. Gandl followed us.

Mid-point along the icy ledges which I have called the arms of the A, the curved surfaces of the sphere became a clutter of smaller ball-like formations—convex scallops within the perfect curve of the circumference.

We asked Gandl if he could explain the meaning of all this.

"Sound caused it," he said. "The sound froze."

It was a vague answer, but I began to see some logic in it. We should have had Professor Peterson with us. He might have carried the explanation much further.

"What do you make of it?" Steve Pound asked me.

"It's a good subject for a painting," I replied. "One of the most interesting studies in form I've ever seen. Look at the zigzag designs running through the ice wherever you break into a cross-section."

Steve was very much annoyed. He continued to mutter that he was not a believer in magic. But he couldn't argue this thing out of existence. For that purpose our little campfire was much more effective. Suddenly there was a cracking and roaring of ice.

I caught glimpses of the glittery fall. Tons of the stuff was crashing downward. Big seams ripped wide and the shrill whistle of the winds blasted our ears.

We rushed out in rough-and-tumble formation, falling and rolling in the snow. By some miracle we escaped the final huge concussion that brought our temple down in a mass of frozen wreckage.

Those irregular blocks of ice were still our friends, however, if we could work fast enough. The blizzard was howling with the promise of freezing us to death. If we could pile the ice blocks together fast enough we might devise a cone-shaped shelter and protect ourselves until there was a chance to get back to the ship. Already Gandl had leaped into the debris of ice to save the fire.

Steve and I worked like snowy demons.

Right around the fire the shelter took form.

A cowardly hope crowded at my mind. If Veeva would only come back and rescue us—or even give us another instantaneous igloo—if it was in her power to do so.

But Steve was much less selfish.

"I hope *she's* not out in this awful storm," he said.

AT length we were again enclosed—this time in a tiny little structure that jabbed our backs and elbows with sharp points of ice. We baked our faces and froze our rears and got our eyes filled with blue smoke. But for the present we were sheltered. I steered our talk back to the instantaneous igloo.

"Did you ever," I asked, "see diagrams of the form which sound waves take?"

I got my sketchbook and drew a few simple illustrations.

"Here," I said, "is an electric bell. Where must you stand to hear it when it rings?"

"Where?" said Steve. "Why anywhere, of course, as long as I'm not too far away."

"The sound waves go out from the point of vibration in a sphere, don't they?"

"I suppose so."

"You know they do. You know that if a train whistles and you've placed a man ten rods north of it, and another ten rods south, another ten east, and another ten west—all four men will hear it at the same time. The same would be true if you were up in the air ten rods above it. That means that every sound vibration tends to spread in the shape of a ball that keeps spreading wider and wider. Now, do you see what might have happened here?"

I pointed to my illustrations, which represented a number of concentric waves growing from the source of the sound.

"If these waves should be caught at a certain point and frozen into something rigid, we would get the exact shape of a sphere."

"How could such a thing happen?"

"I don't know. I only know that the whole structure we had here proves it did happen. Even those smaller inward bulges fit into the same scheme perfectly. Obviously the few waves that struck the banks of ice were bulging back on the rebound—*echoes,* you understand—when the freeze caught them."

Steve nodded. We both looked toward Gandl who shrugged.

"That's better than I could tell it," said Steve, "and don't ask me to explain it when we get back to the ship. Somehow I'd rather we'd just say nothing about it." Then he frowned. "But if it happened once, what's to keep it from happening again?"

"It can," said Gandl. "Whenever the mist is thick it can happen."

"What bothers me is whether Veeva might get trapped too," said Steve.

Gandl replied with a blunt, "No."

More than ever, then, I wondered if the girl had some peculiar power over the sphere of ice. "I think she did it to trap us. We displeased her."

Again we looked at Gandl for any expression that might confirm or reject this new theory.

"You men are my friends," said Gandl. "I must tell you that there are many dangers in this land. You do not know them but I—I have been here before, and Veeva has been here longer than I. She knows all the dangers."

All of us slept. When we awoke, the fire was gone, and the snow was so thick around us that we had to climb the outer walls of our shelter to get up on the surface.

CHAPTER TEN
Invisible Terror

WITHOUT Gandl's help we might have perished.

It was a grueling job, getting back to shore through the deep snow. The treacherous pitfalls were hidden and there were no trails to follow.

But there were landmarks of a sort. We neared the shoreline.

There were three igloos.

Where nothing had been before except the jagged icy banks of a narrow inlet, three spherical snow-covered houses showed white against the black waters.

As we approached the nearest of these we made out the figure of Cedric Peterson.

"The Professor!" I gasped. "What's he doing here?"

"Looking for us, most likely," said Steve, and he called, *"Helloooo—"*

"Sssh!" I gasped. "You'll bring on another one of those things—"

"What things—Oh, you mean—"

"The ice prison, of course. Don't you remember, it was when we were shouting that the thing suddenly came over us."

By that time the Professor was motioning us to be silent. When we got closer he began whispering and pointing to the igloos.

"I dug my way out," he said. "But it was a tough job. I froze six fingers. That spherical wall is all of three feet thick."

The Professor was in bad shape from too much cold. He showed us the mittens he'd worn the ends out of, fighting at the ice.

"I went round and round in the blackness," he said, "before I realized what I was up against."

"How'd it happen?" Steve asked. "Were you yelling at the time?"

"Exactly," said the Professor. "That's what did it. The air is so saturated with moisture that the sound waves crystallized, and there I was, captured by my own voice."

"There are many dangers here," Gandl said dryly.

"We'd better not do any more shouting," Steve warned, holding his voice down to a whisper. Then with a hint of anxiety he said, "Who were you shouting at? Did you see her—the queen?"

"I *thought* I saw her pet tiger," said the Professor. "But on closer inspection I determined that it was a polar bear. And it was at that moment, precisely, that my voice began to function."

Our eyes turned to the other two igloos.

"Was someone with you?"

"The captain and Shorty," said the Professor. "I assume that they are in those two remaining mounds of ice, either frozen to death or slowly going mad like caged animals."

"Come on," said Gandl.

We found a ledge that the snowdrifts had left bare, and it furnished enough stones to serve as tools in our half-frozen hands.

WE BROKE through the second igloo and were rewarded by finding Shorty Barnes, very much alive. In fact, there was the liveliest light in his bulging eyes that I had ever seen.

"They've been chasing me," he whispered in a weird manner. "They've been chasing me all over the place. It was a nightmare."

"Exactly," said the Professor. "A nightmare that would drive any man insane if it went on for long. It's against man's nature to be trapped in the dark."

"Who did it?" Shorty gasped. "Who was that monster?"

"Take it easy, Shorty," said the Professor. "You'll get over those bad dreams before long. Come on, we've got to get Captain French."

We hurried on to the last igloo, and tried to pay no attention to Shorty's erratic mumblings about his delusions of monsters creeping after him in the dark.

As we broke through the two-foot wall of the third igloo, we were greeted by a very unhappy growl.

"The captain!" Shorty said with a sigh. "Come on out, Captain."

Out came a big polar bear. It charged off across the snow.

"Holy smoke," Shorty gasped. He had been on the verge of entering the place. Now he keeled over and fainted.

The polar bear almost got away from us. But Steve had the presence of mind to get a revolver into action. He fired three times, and in the thick twilight we could see the big animal stumble into the snow.

Steve and Gandl made for the beast, and another bullet finished it. Hideous fears were on us now. What had happened to the captain? Had he been caged in with the bear?

We examined the fresh blood that was already freezing around the bear's mouth.

"It could be from the bullet," said Steve, not too confidently. "But if it is, what in the name of heaven happened to Captain French?"

Our balloon of terror was punctured by an angry cry from the second igloo.

"Come here, you damned no-good sailors. What is this, desertion? Or mutiny?"

We raced back to the ice mound from which we had rescued Shorty a few minutes before. Captain French was emerging from it, using the most vigorous language.

We approached him with a chorus of "Sssssh!"

He wasn't a man to be easily quieted, and he was all pent up with rage. He had been neglected and deserted. He thought he had fallen into some curious crevasse, and no one had come to his rescue, and he'd been going round and round trying to keep out of reach of some monstrous animal that he couldn't see in the blackness.

"I didn't dare yell," he whispered hoarsely. "But I didn't lose my head. I puffed and snorted like a mad animal, and I bluffed it out, whatever it was. I think it was a bear."

"It was me," said Shorty.

The captain gave a sullen bark then that would have bluffed out any beast in the arctic, and he commanded that this incident was closed, once and for all and we were never to mention it again.

That brusque command might have stuck, but for one little comment from the Professor which bore deep into the minds of all of us and began twisting and spinning like an icy diamond drill.

"Are we to forget," the Professor said dryly, "that our voices may freeze over us at any moment? There's death in these instantaneous igloos. We've all been lucky to get off this easy."

The captain's gruff rejoinder was not very satisfactory.

"Get a hitch on that bear and let's get back to the ship. As far as Lady Lorruth is to know, we've not been in any special danger. We've all been out on a hunt—"

The captain noticed the faint smile on Gandl's lips, and added hastily.

"I mean a bear hunt."

CHAPTER ELEVEN
Terror Over the Ship

"Sssssh... Ssssssh... Sssssh..." That was the watchword on board the brig during the days that followed.

It was a double-edge hush. Loud talk was dangerous. Unguarded talk could be embarrassing.

For a few days the frightful menace of voices turning to ice was kept secret.

But keeping secrets on a small brig is no easy matter. Our community of wagging tongues and eager ears was too crowded. Every sailor was curious to know whether any of us had seen Veeva. They poo-pooed the idea that we had simply gone on a bear hunt, even though we now had a handsome fur to show for it.

"What, no tigers?" they would say. And the Frabbel brothers added that if *they* had gone hunting they'd have come back with a tiger rug and live prisoner weighed down with gold ornaments.

"No more time for bear hunting," Captain French would argue defensively when the Frabbel brothers began annoying him with their agitations.

"There ought to be a calm before long," Rake Frabbel retorted. "That'll be our chance."

"If any of you damned fly-by-nights go ashore we'll run off and let you freeze to death," the captain said.

"Come on, out with it, Captain," said young Frabbel. And the second brother, Reuben—the one with cheek-whiskers that reached up to the bags under his eyes—joined the hecklers and climbed on the band wagon with an offer to bet a hundred dollars that the captain had already paid his respects to that "damned fetching ice lady."

"You want to bet?" the captain snarled.

"Only I ain't got a hundred dollars," said Reuben Frabbel with a taunting grin.

Meanwhile Lady Lucille was being as suspicious as a caged cat about twenty-four hours a day. And there the captain was finding himself in hot water aplenty.

"You'd be surprised," Professor Peterson confided to me, "how the old boy has been arguing with Lady Lorruth. He insists we shouldn't try to go on searching for her husband, unless we first pick up every scrap of information from those we pass."

Our conversation broke off shortly. *The girl was coming across the horizon, riding like the wind.*

PROFESSOR PETERSON and I, standing on the starboard deck, were the first to see her—we thought. The shore was a quarter of a mile away, and there was a light mist; but we couldn't mistake the figures with the whirlwind of flying snow following in their wake.

"Look!" the Professor gulped. I cupped my hands to my mouth as if to *shout* to her. "Don't," he snapped. "Wait. Don't make a sound."

Girl and tiger galloped on across the white land, paralleling our course, making at least twice our speed. She made no effort to hail us. Rather, it appeared, she merely intended to keep abreast our progress.

Captain caught sight of her, and you could see the shudder that passed over him. He was bending over the rail at the prow, and had been supervising a job of mending an ugly ice gouge in the hull. Below him were the three Frabbel brothers in the dory, bouncing along beside the ship. The captain had given them this repair job to shut them up, I think. Certainly not because they were carpenters. And not because it was agreeable weather for such work. It was only nine degrees above zero.

Young Frabbel noticed that the captain was looking off in the distance intently, and the husky young sailor turned.

He must have seen the girl just before she disappeared. The hammer slipped from his hand and splashed into the sea. And young Frabbel suddenly yelled—a shrieking note calculated to wake the high heavens.

He must have yelled again. I saw him yell. *But I didn't hear.*

In the split second after his lips parted, it happened.

A huge spherical chunk of ice appeared against the side of the hull. It was like an immense white balloon bulging out through the ship. Less than a third of it was visible.

Then it turned and slushed into the water—a rounded chunk of ice with a sheer side that edged up out of the water. The overturned dory was caught within, and its keel could barely be seen through the dark green water.

The three Frabbels were somewhere inside that broken ball of ice. The object began to drift away from the ship, through the waves of green-black paint.

We worked fast. The captain's orders were sometimes helpful, more often superfluous. It was a job that challenged every man who could throw a hook.

Presently the chunk of ice was spinning back toward us, and we could see that Reuben Frabbel was coming out of the trap alive. His arms were waving, but his legs were held fast between the dory and the ice.

Gandl and Steve and four others braved the icy water. When they came back, many minutes later, with the aid of our ropes, they had done all that any men could have done...

Again the dory hung in its place on the foredeck.

And again, after three or four days, the voices of the Frabbel brothers were added to the noise of those rooms astern where cursing and obscene talk flourished.

But now there were two Frabbel brothers, not three. Rake, the oldest, had been buried at sea...

Lady Lucille rang the assembly bell and in her most vitriolic manner she gave us a dressing down.

"From now on," she said, "this ship is going to be under the sternest of discipline."

Then and there she authorized the captain to apply severe punishment—chains or worse—for any offenders.

I WENT away from this session with mingled awe and amusement. It was marvelous to see how uncertain of ourselves and of the expedition every man of us had become. Peril hovered around us. The sounds of clattering dishes, of slamming doors, of ringing bells—any noise whatsoever was taken as ominous.

This fear was a growing thing—like the fear that multiplies in a mob. And, strange to say, the new stillness was as much a reminder of the terror as any noise.

Shorty was the one who did the most talking about these strange ice traps.

"They might hit us any time," he would whisper. "They come just like that out of thin air."

He snapped his fingers.

"And do you know what would happen? The whole ship would be covered by a great big ball of ice—tons of it—and over we'd go."

His eyes would almost bug out of their sockets. In a picture it would have been funny. But I wasn't in the mood to draw any caricatures.

All of this talk was maddening to Lady Lucille Lorruth.

To add to her visions of hideous disaster Steve Pound and Gandl made another short excursion over to the island coast. They returned with stories that reinforced Shorty's calamity howling. They had sighted a dozen or more various-sized ice mounds that dotted one side of a deep V-shaped valley.

These wild terrors crystallized into a strict silence. Lady Lorruth had me make dozens of signs to post around on all corners of the ship.

"Make no noise." "Do not speak above a whisper."

CHAPTER TWELVE
Whisperings of Romance

THERE was a humorous side to all this whispering.

Terror is one thing; attraction for a beautiful girl is quite another. The sailors chose to believe that these ice-traps were a phenomenon of fogs and mists, and that this mysterious creature named Veeva had nothing to do with them.

And so, while we were stalled again by a dead calm, the boys began to cast longing eyes toward the shore.

The girl must be following us for some reason. Perhaps she had a favorite on board. One after another the seamen began to spruce up. Young Frabbel began shaving and sometimes went so far as to wash his face.

Looking back upon this now, I must admit that I was developing my own delusion the same as the others. I began telling myself that I might be the lucky man who would gain this girl's favor. Hadn't she rescued me with her own hands?

I had always supposed I would marry some day. It was just one of those things I had never got around to. At any rate I began planning and wondering and scheming. This girl was too beautiful to be left living in this arctic wilderness.

How interesting it would be to her to come back to New York! But in this dream I always came to a dead stop when I remembered that *she was a queen.*

Queen of what?

Was she really a person of royal blood? Did she maintain responsibilities toward some little kingdom of Greenland natives?

I must see her again soon.

Now and then our vigilance of watching for her was rewarded—we would catch glimpses of the girl riding along over the icy hills; as Reuben Frabbel put it, "Within rifle range, only who gives a damn about a white tiger?"

Those rare glimpses were what gave zest to the long hours of the dark winter, now on us.

BY THIS time we had all come to look to Gandl for authoritative information. Would this girl continue to follow us? Was she really a queen? Were there villages to supply her with food and shelter? Did she know this whole terrain?

Gandl was living in Shorty's room now, and Shorty would come to me to complain.

"They're overworking Gandl," he said. "One man after another comes to him to ask confidential questions. And they all ask the same silly things. Is she already married? And if she is, where's her husband? What's he the king of? Is he a good fighter? Does he have firearms?"

Even the captain, Shorty said, would make these inquiries. But about all anyone got out of Gandl was that she was a queen.

IN OUR general discussions the dominating note would be dangers that we all knew could strike upon us at any time—the certainty that our ship could be capped with a sphere of ice and instantly overturned and sunk.

The arctic winter came on us in earnest now. We came to a dead stop. All our prying and tugging at hooks and bars and anchors was to no avail. The shelf ice slipped down against us from the north. It crowded in under the bow of the ship and upended us. It crashed against the sides of the hull. Foot by foot we were elevated until we sat, high and dry, upon the thick, solid floor.

We were one with the distant land. We saw that we could walk toward the mountains, north, east, or south, without ever having to cross any waters. The waters were gone. Continents and islands were joined in one endless plain of ice.

You may have read of arctic expeditions in which such an imprisonment has brought on months of despair. Such was not the case with us. On the contrary. And the reason was Veeva. Everyone interested in her was secretly or openly elated over the plight of our ship. The ocean barrier between us and this glorious Viking beauty had been removed.

Days without apparent dangers had made for lax enforcement of the whispering rule. And now the captain yielded to pressure and sanctioned a few brief hunting expeditions.

Hunting suddenly became the popular sport—we called it polar bear hunting or seal hunting. Or, in the case of the captain, it was a scouting expedition to look for reindeers. But the important news from these expeditions became a matter of open interest—had anyone seen Veeva?

But once Steve Pound went hunting alone *and didn't come back*.

A terrific blizzard set in and hung on for five days, and no rescue party dared go out more than three-quarters of a mile from the ship. The thermometer dropped to below zero, and three sailors who had started off on the rescue mission were dragged back half dead.

When the storm's fury was over, we made further efforts to comb the base of the mountain for signs of a lost man.

Finally we knew we were beaten. And still we waited, hour after hour, always expecting—

But Steve Pound did not return.

CHAPTER THIRTEEN
The Lady Borrows a Knife

MY WORK kept me on board ship. Lady Lucille was becoming more demanding. I had to work outside in some of that bitter weather. I could sketch for only a few minutes at a time.

Sometimes there was moonlight to highlight the contours of the icy mountains. Sometimes there were glorious northern lights and crackling electric storms that crept close to the surface. These were the features of the arctic night, which Lady Lorruth wanted me to capture in my paintings.

In her commands to all of us she was becoming exceedingly caustic and bitter. Her nerves were overwrought. Her eyes were forever shifting. She had lost the confidence of the crew long ago. Worse, she was losing that of Captain French.

She knew, too, that the men were talking about her.

"What are they saying?" she asked me in private one morning.

"How do I know, when they speak in whispers?" I replied.

"They wonder why I've come here, don't they? They doubt my—my purpose for this expedition."

"I hope they have no reason to do that," I said. "But you're the only one who truly knows what that reason is."

Her lips tightened. "I'm going to make you a gift, Jim," she said. "I'll give you several valuable furs—some of the finest. But you must...*talk*...to the crew for me. Tell them I'm still yearning for the love of my husband. Tell them I still have faith that he isn't dead. Make them believe it, Jim. Don't let them think I've only come to...to claim his treasures..." She then paused and looked at me with a steely look in her eyes. "But when we do find them—and we will—they're mine, Jim. *Mine*. Do you understand?"

"Of course they're yours, Lady Lorruth—"

"Say it again, Jim. Say it again, and don't look at me in that accusing way..."

It was pitiful to listen to her. This matter was burning into her soul. The more she talked the more she revealed that she was sure her husband was dead and that she was glad of it. Of course I could say nothing to the crew, for everyone knew by this time that one of her highest hopes was to find the wealth of furs. And a perfectly natural and rightful hope it was—except for the fact that she was glad her husband was dead.

Another high hope was to marry into Captain French's fortune.

This truth became apparent to all of us.

But an awful fear was obstructing her plan. Her second goal was growing more remote. *Captain French was losing interest in her.*

Upon one pretext or another, the captain had discontinued those comradely walks around the deck with her. And now the spark of truth was igniting her proud fury.

The captain, along with the common deck hands, had become somewhat enamored with the Queen of the Ice.

This left Lady Lorruth with her first hope only—the finding of the furs. From day to day I could sense the intensifying of her passion to find the lost furs.

ON another occasion she said to me, "I know Lord Lorruth has left an enormous amount of furs for me—somewhere. We will find them. We *must* find them. You can imagine how my people back in England will treat me when I return. This could make me one of the wealthier women in the British Isles."

"That will be wonderful," I said, trying to match her enthusiasm.

"And then Captain French will be…envious…don't you think?"

"I—I suppose so."

"I'm sure he will. Men like Captain French aren't easily swerved by trifles, are they?"

"Why, no—er—you know Captain French's stout-hearted character as well as I."

I was groping for these comments. Her arguments bore down upon me so insistently that I felt compelled to agree with her. On the occasions when I dared controvert her observations she would fly into a huff and stalk into her room, sometimes slamming the door behind her.

Whether I should have pampered her or not, I do not know.

"Yes…Captain French will see me in a very different light," she said. She looked off into the distance, a strange smile on her face and a faraway look in her eyes. "He will be taken in with envy—perhaps even jealousy—and then he will come to me and remind me of our old friendship."

There was a pregnant pause. Then she turned and looked directly at me.

"And do you think I will marry him then?"

This one I could not possibly answer. But before I could reply she had her own answer.

"Not unless he apologizes for every moment of neglect. These are painful hours that I'm enduring, Jim. For every hour of his infidelity through this winter night I will demand many hours of apology." She laughed nervously and looked off into the distance again. "Perhaps I should make him apologize to me on his knees."

These fancies gave her eyes an underlying glow of sadistic delight.

Something Steve Pound had said to me kept humming through my brain. "Lady Lucille is going a little crazy." That is what Steve had thought.

I watched her intently as she stood there, twisting a corner of paper on my drawing board into shreds.

"He'll come back to me. Perhaps even he'll crawl back. Yes...yes, he'll crawl on his hands and look up to me with envious, pleading eyes. He'll sing his apologies in every key."

"And then?"

"And then—ahhh!"

"You'll—you'll marry him?"

"Perhaps," she said, "if it suits my pleasure. Or I may—yes, I may stab him through the heart."

Her eyes were fixed upon a small putty knife that I used for cleaning dried paint off the palette. The object fascinated her and her nervous fingers began to play upon the handle.

"Do you need this?" she said with a sudden change to a matter-of-fact mood.

"Frequently, yes."

"I'd like to borrow it," she said brightly. "My window keeps frosting over, and a case knife's no good."

"Very well."

It was Professor Peterson who called my attention that evening to the fact that Lady Lorruth was sharpening this little putty knife on a soapstone.

"More idiosyncrasies," I muttered.

"She'll bear watching," he said.

WITHIN twenty-four hours everyone was talking about her strange conduct. Professor Peterson thought I had better go to her and ask for my property. I was glad to comply. She met me at the door of her cabin and instantly I found myself on the defensive. Her manner was imperious.

"Please tell Captain French to call an assembly," she said.

Again I obeyed. We assembled on the east deck, which was partially roofed over by shelf ice that had crowded over the bulwarks and settled.

There was considerable tension as we lined up. Shorty was perspiring in spite of the sub-zero temperature.

Lady Lorruth stated her demands with a minimum of words.

"I want my furs. I want every fur that Lord Lorruth has left for me. Somewhere there is an enormous cache—his last communications indicated this. You should have found it before this. I'm feeding you and paying you. There's no more time to waste. I want you to find this cache as quickly as is humanly possible."

Captain French broke in with a blustering protest.

"How can we? We're still fifteen miles from the place you said we'd find another cache."

"So what do you intend to do?"

Captain French stammered. "We'll wait till the ice breaks away, of course, and finish our voyage."

"You'll do nothing of the sort. You'll set out on foot. Equip yourselves as necessary."

"Fifteen miles in this temperature?"

"Those are my orders. I will endure this agony of waiting no longer. I simply won't tolerate another day without these riches—riches that are rightfully mine."

"I'm telling you, Lady Lucille," the captain's face was white. "We're not working this right. If we want to find out what happened, we've got to contact these people."

He made an indefinite gesture toward the eastern mountains.

"*These* people? *What* people?"

"You know—there are people out there somewhere. We've seen—"

"We've seen *one*," said Lady Lucille bitterly. "That awful female. But she's not a person. She's a phantasm—an evil spirit—a curse!"

A curse! The word struck home. It caught us off guard.

"*You* know I'm right, Cedric Peterson," she stormed. You've read that book on the workings of maledictions!"

Professor Peterson faltered, "Yes, but I—"

Lady Lucille followed her advantage. "And you, Malonski, you'll bear me out that these curses still work today."

"Well, that one time I told you about—" Malonski began timidly.

"They *do* work. This female spirit is following us, haunting us. I forbid any of you to see her again."

Captain French's dark face trembled and he began muttering angrily. A moment later the two of them were arguing loudly. Captain French insisted that the one sensible thing to do was to find this "Ice Queen" and obtain from her any information she had regarding Lord Lorruth.

The meeting ended in a tense deadlock and a bizarre exhibition of behavior by Lady Lorruth. She was fairly screaming by now, even hurling threats. We were awed, not so much by her threats as by her insane manner.

"I'll cut the heart out of the first man who dares to speak with that diabolical siren. I don't care which one of you it is. I tell you that woman has placed a curse upon my husband and upon us. Give heed to my words. It will be *death* for anyone of you who *speaks* to her—even you, Jim McClurg, or you, Cedric Peterson, or you—you—you—"

She was screaming at the top of her voice now. With trembling fingers she was pointing at Captain French, who actually backed off a few steps. I'm sure the entire crew was paralyzed with fear at the thought of an ice bubble forming over the entire ship, which—inexplicably—did not happen.

In that sickening moment, as the captain was backing away from her and we were all cringing at this terrible exhibition of madness, a flurry of sleet and snow to the east of our ship caught our attention.

We turned and stared through our barricade of ice. *Veeva, the Queen, was riding toward us.*

CHAPTER FOURTEEN
A Party for Nobility

IT WAS the strangest meeting that I've ever witnessed. The tiger stopped with his forepaws on the ship's rail. Veeva the beautiful was before us, her eyes flashing boldness, her lips laughing. She was sitting sidesaddle, and her bare legs were brown against the tiger's coat of snowy white.

"Hello," Veeva greeted.

None of us could speak without disobeying Lucille's commands. But I smiled and nodded, and I noticed that several others did the same.

I expected Lady Lucille to burst into a fit of violence. Her hysteria was beyond the point of recovery. She seemed ready to fly into a torrent of irrational screaming.

But no, she was past words. Instead, she drew from the inside pocket of her coat my putty knife. It flashed up in her hands and she started forward.

Icy terror ran through my spine.

Matching Veeva's fierce beauty was her dazzling metal accoutrements. She wore on her side an ornamental sword and this she seized without an instant's hesitation.

At the same time she emitted one of her boisterous laughs, gurgling and irrepressible. It proved that this whole terrifying situation was no threat to make her heart quail. To her it was simply a ridiculous bluff.

"Come on, Lady, let's play that we're having a duel," Veeva shouted with glee.

Then her rippling laughter ran up and down the scales. She slapped the tiger on the throat and it bounded down off the ship and out to a little plaza of ice. Veeva leaped nimbly to her feet.

"Come on," she cried again. "We'll let my tiger be the referee."

The big pet gave a fierce growl.

Poor Lady Lorruth! Her upraised arm went stiff. She was mad enough to kill. But her helplessness was obvious. She turned and stomped into her cabin. The door closed with a solid bang.

Would the captain dare to speak to Veeva?

Professor Peterson and I were the ones who chanced a violation of Lady Lucille's stout restriction.

"Where's Steve Pound?" I asked. "Have you seen him anywhere?"

"You could help us, Veeva," the professor said. "You could tell us what we need to know. You saw that terrible demonstration. The woman is going mad. But if you could show us the way we might save her."

"What do you want?" Veeva asked.

"We want news of Lord Lorruth and his fur trading expedition. They came here five years ago. They were supposed to have reached a point fifty miles north of here. We're sure that they came this far. We found a letter. We believe there's a treasure cache—"

The captain interrupted with a challenging bark.

"And we want to know where you got those furs you are wearing."

PROFESSOR PETERSON tried to soften the tone of the conversation. "Your furs are your own business, of course. You needn't answer personal questions unless you wish. But about Lord Lorruth—"

"And Steve Pound," I put in.

The girl gave one of her amused laughs. "I needn't answer any questions."

Professor Peterson turned to the captain. "This lady is a queen. She deserves the finest hospitality that we can offer. Why do we allow her to stand out there on the ice? Can't we persuade her to come and eat at our table? Isn't it time for a party? We could serve a double ration of grog."

The captain stammered and stumbled. The suggestion embarrassed him. His authority was being slowly consumed between two fires—the madness of Lady Lucille, and the cool rationality of Professor Peterson.

But the suggestion of an extra drink struck the captain at his weakest point.

The girl came aboard.

The tiger waited at a safe distance.

We all sat together at a table. Though it was a meager feast, the spirit was convivial, for we had no trouble persuading the captain that the occasion merited an extra measure of drink all around.

But the joviality was strained. Steve Pound was no longer with us. He had been one of Veeva's foremost friends and champions. Now she cunningly evaded every question that any of us tried to ask about him.

And there were more immediate reasons for the nerve-strain that attended our party. I kept an eye on the dining room door fearing that Lady Lorruth might enter at any moment. Perhaps she had swooned in a fit of insanity. If so, this meeting might succeed in forming the confidence we needed.

But the captain was over-eager, and Gandl sat moodily silent. As often as Professor Peterson and I would be ready to pop an important question, something would be sure to break down the rapport we had established.

Finally Professor Peterson went out, dragging Shorty along with him. A little later Shorty came back and told me the professor wanted to see me.

Out of hearing of the others, Professor Peterson said, "We'll call each of the men out one at a time. They've got to understand our tactics. Veeva *is* a queen. She may be the queen of some insignificant village of twenty-five natives, or she may be the ruling power over some worldwide secret society. You never can tell. At any rate, we've got to mobilize our efforts to bolster this reception. She's a person of majesty. In her own eyes she may be far more important than Lady Lucille Lorruth. We'll treat her accordingly."

I said, "It sounds like insubordination."

"It is," said the professor, "but it makes good sense."

AND so one after the other of us came back from Professor Peterson's little curtain lecture, and gradually the whole atmosphere of the whole party changed.

"We must stop for a toast," I said, lifting my glass. "It is the rarest of privileges to drink to a queen, and I'm sure we all agree that she is the world's most beautiful."

We drank and applauded, and Professor Peterson said that now it was time for us to bow. So we all bowed.

"When my friends bow to me," said Veeva, glowing with pleasure, "I sing them this little song."

She sang a funny little melody with words we couldn't understand. Then she laughed and we got up and, after Professor Peterson had seated her most courteously, we all sat again.

We ceased to bombard her with our rapid-fire questions that had made her take refuge in evasion. And she was beginning to talk to us of her own free will.

Unfortunately Lady Lucille appeared at the door in time to spoil everything.

Professor Peterson did his best to draw a curtain over the early scene of near-violence.

"We take pleasure, Queen Veeva," the professor bowed low to the girl, "in presenting to you Lady Lucille Lorruth."

Veeva smiled and responded with sparkling interest. "I'm very pleased, Lady Lucille. Is the term Lady not a title of distinction?"

Lady Lorruth answered coldly, "It's a title of nobility."

The reply was blunt and hard as an iceberg.

"Whatever your line of nobility may be," Veeva smiled, "I am happy to recognize it."

"My native England is one of the oldest nations in the world," said Lady Lucille proudly. "There is nothing in the North American hemisphere to approach it for age or importance."

"This is news to me," said Veeva. And she was growing serious. "Are you talking in terms of hundreds of centuries or thousands?"

Lady Lucille shrugged and turned to the captain. "What does she mean hundreds of centuries? Our time can only be counted in terms of sixty centuries."

"Yes, of course," the captain said, eager to reinforce Lady Lucille on what he considered to be a sure point of knowledge. "Two thousand years takes us back to the time of Christ. Four thousand more takes us to the beginning of time. All this counts up to—ah—er—about sixty centuries I believe."

The curiosity in Veeva's eyes was a picture. She looked from one to the other of use as if to say, "Do all of you agree? Is this your conception of time?"

But her answer was highly polite. "My highest respect to you, and to your subjects, Lady Lucille. Your modern outlook upon this world is most refreshing."

THE captain was ready to change the subject. "About those furs—"

"Oh, yes, those furs," said Veeva. "You all seem to be very much agitated. What is the difficulty?"

"I want my furs," said Lady Lucille. "My husband came here five years ago. He came for furs, but he didn't return with them. They're here in this land, and I want them."

"Five years, ago?" Veeva reflected. "It seems but yesterday. I think I can lead you to the cache where the treasure has been deposited."

"Good," Lady Lucille snapped. "We'll go at once."

"But the way is perilous. I'm sorry that I can't carry more than one or two extra passengers on my tiger. I advise you to stay with the ship, Lady Lucille."

Lady Lucille didn't take kindly to the suggestion.

"How far is it?" the captain asked. "Do we have to cross those mountains?"

151

"The trail winds through a valley," said Veeva. "But why be afraid? I'll lead you."

There was a long tense silence. Bitter suspicions in Lady Lucille's eyes were feasting upon the girl.

"Would you take me?" Lady Lucille asked.

Veeva smiled. "Could you endure crossing the dangerous glacier? Could you—"

"I see through you," Lady Lucille broke in angrily. "You're coaxing me to go so you can hurl me off a cliff or some other treacherous act."

"Was I coaxing you?" Veeva laughed.

"You know I would never get back alive. You want to steal what is mine."

Veeva's laughter subsided with a flush of embarrassment. Her eyes blazed with a will to fight but she held her temper. There was a hint of mockery in her fierce smile.

"Such talk! Are you truly a Lady of nobility?"

"Where did you get those furs you're wearing?" Lady Lucille said with increasing loudness. "I think you just may be a thief. My husband left me some special red fox—" And on and on she raved.

Veeva was bewildered that we should all sit there in helpless silence as if used to hearing such talk. She couldn't understand whether this was some kind of a game or some misunderstanding. Smiling, she refused to take it as a brutal insult, for had we not been treating her to honors?

"Do you indulge your nobility in these fancies as a sport...? I must be going."

Many of us instantly pleaded for her to stay. We tried to apologize for our Lady Lucille's conduct. The conference turned into pandemonium. Everyone was talking.

WHILE we tried to straighten matters out, some of us were playing our own personal games, trying to gain a word of favor from Veeva.

But the insults had sunken in by now, and they could not be undone. Veeva walked briskly to the door.

She turned and quieted us with a stinging speech.

"I have had enough of your silly nobility. It carries no weight with me. Your race is too young and raw to have any pride. My own race is as old as these mountains. I have been the queen for thousands of years. I can't be annoyed by a little passing rudeness. *So soon you will all be gone!*"

"Gone?" Lady Lucille echoed. "Gone?" She repeated it over and over like a crazy parrot caught by a single word.

"In three or four centuries," said Veeva, "you may have more reason for pride. If so, come back to me again—or send your great-grandchildren. I will still be here, riding these icy mountains."

We stood there gaping. No one knew what to say.

Veeva herself gave us our cue.

"Bow to me, if any of you are still my friends... Bow to the Queen of the Ice."

I bowed and the deepest of reverence was in my gesture. I do not know how many of the others bowed. When my eyes lifted I saw Veeva riding away in a flurry of snow.

CHAPTER FIFTEEN
A Valley Under a Roof

"I'LL follow her," said Shorty. Within the next half-hour as many as a dozen of us left the ship and started the uncertain trek across the field of ice.

We started together. But soon we had split into several groups, and some of the slower ones turned back.

Shorty and Professor Peterson and I managed to keep pace with Gandl, who had agreed to lead us part way.

It was a darkened world, but there was a bright glow from the stars, and the white snow had left a good trail. Our course led in a wide semicircle back to the south.

"That looks like the same valley we saw from another direction—Steve and I," said Professor Peterson. "I can see some of the same ice-mounds."

His eyes were better than mine. Even with his telescope I had difficulty spotting that row of ice domes. Our panorama took in a wide semicircular valley with black patches of mountains showing through the vast humps of blue snow.

The trail was fresher with each hour of travel, until at last we knew that Veeva must be riding only a short distance ahead of us.

We were tempted to call. But we remembered, and plowed on in comparative silence.

At last we overtook her.

She was waiting at the entrance of a deep crevasse. As soon as we were close enough for her to identify us she cried her greetings. But the remark she addressed to Gandl was brief and mysterious.

"You...? I'm surprised."

We followed in her wake and found ourselves descending between vertical walls about five feet apart. The footing was perilous. A little stream of water slid over the smooth blue ice. The canyon rose high above us. Its depth was hard to gauge. I remember looking up and guessing that we were two hundred feet beneath the tops of the walls.

This fissure must have been formed by a very sudden break in the backbone of ice many years ago. The walls showed signs of much weathering. Countless footmarks of the tiger were embedded in the irregular floor upon which we were traveling.

This was delightful. After these many weeks of looking down on fields of ice, this was like a new world. My eyes were seeing colors that they had forgotten, streaks of purple mingled with the straight hard surfaces of blue, which rose in frozen sheets on either side of us.

Sometimes we could hear trickling waterfalls or the low roar of rivers beneath the glaciers. And Veeva would pause to tell us of the vastness of these wonders we could not see, as if she knew them all.

I lost all sense of direction, almost all sense of time. We stopped occasionally for food and rest. This journey must have taken two days or more. We were still descending.

"And you are still coming, Gandl?" Veeva would say each time she waited for us to catch up.

"I am very much with you, still," Gandl might answer. Or perhaps he would only nod and look intently at her, with the bright fire blazing in his eyes.

AT length our tunnel widened into a sort of reception room. There were signs of habitation here. The floor had been backed with stones in somewhat regular formation. Light somehow reflected down through the irregular icy formations overhead.

They were like massive chandeliers. They added to our sense of wonderment. But they were of deadly peril. As we proceeded along this wide reception room a freak crash would thunder against our ears. Then we would see through the blue reflections that one of these mammoth icicles had fallen. Our hearts beat faster. Death threatened our every step.

An hour later our way came upon steps hewn in the stone. There must have been thousands of them.

At this point Veeva's tiger wanted to run and she had trouble holding him back.

Shorty had almost passed out from fatigue. He was given the privilege of riding. How I envied him. The professor was following along back of me.

Abruptly he called to Veeva. "What happened to Gandl?"

We all turned and our eyes tried to penetrate the gloomy blue darkness. Far back, high on the steps we could make out the figure of Gandl. He had stopped and was settling himself in a comfortable position against the stone wall.

We called to him and urged him to come on.

"What's the matter?" I shouted. "Are you exhausted?"

At this his laugh echoed mysteriously down through the narrow pass.

Veeva said, "He doesn't want to come. Leave him alone."

We proceeded on our journey. But I felt uneasy, going ahead without Gandl. And Veeva kept looking back through the long narrow stairway until our way leveled off and turned in a new direction.

Now that the footing was solid I trudged along almost unconsciously. I think I fell asleep while walking.

Awakening, I was aware that Shorty and Veeva were still carrying on a conversation in low tones, barely audible above the noise of our footsteps.

Shorty was observing the bright-colored stones, imagining there were all sorts of precious gems in this unexplored region. Then I seemed to fall asleep again and came to consciousness only when the sounds of other voices seeped in upon my hearing.

Everything was so utterly dark. I could hardly believe that I was not in the midst of some grotesque dream. But my sore feet were still pounding along over a hard path of ice or stone, and my aching muscles were no dream.

I rubbed my eyes. My sight adjusted to the strange dark light, not like any I had ever experienced before. It was iridescence that glowed from the very walls and the floor, from every promontory of stone.

This was no longer darkness. But it was utterly unlike sunlight. As I became used to it the effect was highly pleasing. The dim rocks took on a variety of colors—some of them shadowy, others scintillating against black backgrounds.

Shorty and the professor were silent. They were also drinking in the fairyland beauty of the passing scene.

What attracted me most was a long row of black dots running horizontally along the wall. The design was simple. When we came close enough to this continuous border I rubbed my gloved hand along to discover that it was made up of a series of gouges which had been cut into the living stone.

The murmur of distant voices grew louder. At length I began to see the shadows of many people in the distance. I whispered to Peterson.

"Where are we? What does it mean?"

"A lost world!" the professor whispered. "Some runaway branch of humanity that has hidden itself away."

"There must be hundreds of them."

"Or thousands!"

It was like nothing anyone had ever dreamed—that a colony of human beings could be living deep under a glacier.

I wished for Steve Pound. What would he have thought? Perhaps his hardheaded outlook, his commonsense knowledge would have been insulted.

But I was eager, now, for all my eyes could take in. Even though my mind tried to reject it.

Rivers ran along beside our path. Occasionally we saw what appeared to be gardens. We could smell fresh green plant life and the brilliance of the plants were like emeralds.

We saw small four-wheeled wagons being pushed into little branch caverns that must have been mines.

We passed a group of workmen who were sitting in a circle eating from metal dishes. They were wearing light garments of furs. Their leaders wore special ornaments, including a Viking helmet and bracelets that might have been gifts from some old Norsemen.

These people must have been well adjusted to the coolness of their climate. Many of them were not wearing gloves. They were going about their work casually; to them this was obviously the normal manner of living.

A group of girls, crossing our trail ahead of us, stopped to bow to Queen Veeva—and they were happy and proud in doing so.

But our appearance caused great interest and curiosity among all these people. As we passed on, they broke into excited jabbering in a language we could not understand.

Veeva dropped a few explanations along the way.

"Your manner of talking is comparatively new to us down here," she said. "Many of my people have not had the chance to study it. But I, the Queen, must know all languages. So must the Firemakers. Otherwise, how would we know how to deal with our prisoners?"

"Prisoners?" Shorty gulped, turning chalk-white.

Veeva smiled proudly. "Only with this most indispensable tool, *language,* was I able to deal properly with your friend Lord Lorruth when he and his party trespassed on my hunting ground."

"Then he's here?" I blurted. "He's your prisoner?"

"For life," said Veeva merrily. "Wouldn't you like to join him?"

CHAPTER SIXTEEN
Cells for Enemies

"THESE people you see," Veeva continued, "are preparing to harvest these crops. Ever since our nation took refuge in the caverns under the ice we have managed to cultivate a goodly quantity of grains and vegetables. From the streams we get our meat, and also from the ice fields high over our heads."

Beyond a high triangular doorway we saw a tall gaunt man, clad in ornamental furs, walking along in a manner of great importance. He was being attended by six boys. He would send any of them on errands to make stone marks on a mound of ice at the foot of the wall. They would come and go at his beck and call.

Then he would stop and instruct them. His language was this same conglomeration of sounds that didn't fit into any foreign tongue I had ever heard. Suddenly he veered into English and I caught his words, and we paused to listen. He was too intent on his task to notice us.

"Hear me, boys," he said. "This is the new *code* of our enemies. If you would walk from our world into theirs they would greet you with words like these. Do you understand me?"

Some of the boys understood, others asked to have the words repeated. The tall man went over his statements carefully.

"You see," he said, "our enemy knows that we have learned some of their codes, so they must change their style of talk. They do this so they can confuse us. But if we know their new code we will understand their plans to kill us."

At this point Veeva called out to the tall dignitary. "Hello there, could the enemy spies understand you if they were listening?"

The tall man jerked about in great surprise. Our presence disconcerted him. His mouth moved nervously and his black broom-straw beard waggled, but for a moment he couldn't speak in our code or any other. He struggled to recover himself and took a few steps toward Veeva.

"Our beloved Queen!" He bowed low and the six boys surrounding him followed his example.

"Arise, Firemaker," Veeva said. The tall man came to his feet. The boys remained in a kneeling position.

"We welcome you. If I had known you were coming, a celebration would have been ready."

The tall man bowed again. Then he and the boys arose.

"Conduct me to the Red Room," said Veeva.

"You will not first go to the King?"

"I think not, Firemaker," said Veeva. "Is he still sleeping?"

"Of course," the Firemaker replied. "If you have been up among the mountains and skies, you should know whether he will go on sleeping. Is the sun shining yet?"

"No," said Veeva.

"Just as I thought," said the Firemaker. "The enemies have not departed, so the king will go on sleeping."

Veeva agreed with this, apparently, although she seemed unworried by this mysterious enemy.

Shorty interrupted to ask what kind of people these enemies were and where they came from.

"Where did *you* come from?" Veeva rejoined. "What kind of people are *you?*"

For some reason this confused conversation made me feel that I was on my way to be hanged. If so, I would be an easy victim, for I was already half-dead from exhaustion.

I was placed in a cell by myself.

OF the ceremony that followed, I saw little. I could hear the sound. I could catch echoes of curious folk songs. And when my eyes looked across the vast expanse of colored light that was obviously the Red Room, I could catch glimpses of the shadowy figures of these natives moving through their weird dances.

I'm glad to say that the temperatures, which prevailed overhead, had been escaped. Here the air was warm and drowsy. Soon after I had been locked in the cell I went off to sleep.

That sleep must have extended over many hours. I awakened intermittently. The metal dishes of food placed before me were delicious. Food and sleep—what luxury. But after my strength returned I was angry with myself, for failing to watch the native ceremonies.

At last my siege of snoozing was over. I roused up and sauntered to the doorway of my cell.

The curious light, which I have already described, seemed to come from every surface of stone. My room was a high-ceilinged prison about twenty feet in circumference. The single doorway was closed by means of a huge slab of rock, which had been carved through with long narrow ornamental slits.

There must have been several such cells. To my right, in a semicircular alcove, I could see five or six of these doorways, all of them prisons.

I suddenly caught echoes of a low conversation within a few feet of me. I recognized the voice of Shorty.

"We could go into a circus," he was saying. "I'd be a trick rider in no time."

Then I heard the low laughter of Veeva. My pulse jumped. I crowded against my stone door, trying to see. But Shorty's cell door must have been flush with mine. I listened.

"You'd be surprised," Shorty said, "how much money we could make, and we'd be famous too, and we'd wear yellow tights and everybody would shout and clap and whistle for us."

Veeva answered. Something that I couldn't hear.

Then the low conversation came from a different cell, and I knew that she was talking with Professor Peterson. She was simply inquiring about his health and comfort, so far as I could gather.

PRESENTLY Veeva came to me. Her beautiful face was at the doorway. Through the grill of carved stone her beautiful eyes were smiling upon me.

My resolution to declare my love faltered. Had she come to mock and ridicule? Wasn't she barely repressing her quick laughter?

But no, her eyes were gazing at me intently. She said in a low serious voice, "Are you quite comfortable, Jim McClurg?"

"Frankly, no. I want to get out of here."

"Have you had food and rest?" she asked.

"Yes, I'm ready for a journey back out. When do we go?"

"Why do you want to go back?" she asked.

"I don't feel safe," I retorted. "For all I know, the cell may crumble down on me at any moment. I don't know your people. They make me nervous—all their music and jabber, and their big fierce faces."

"Are you afraid of them?"

"Yes."

"You're very suspicious," she said, reaching through the stone bars to press my hand. "I would be glad to acquaint you with this world, but I must tell you at once, forget all about going back. Drop it from your thoughts."

I felt very much like a trapped animal.

I didn't want to suspect Veeva of treachery. It's very difficult to gaze upon a girl so beautiful and think evil of her. I somehow controlled my rising temper, but only because there was a scheme in the back of my mind.

"How long have you lived here?" I asked.

"All my life."

"How far away have you been?"

"Many miles," she said. "Even many weeks' journey, traveling with Whitey. I know all of the coasts and all of the mountains."

"Have you ever been down into Labrador?"

Her silence was as good as a negative answer. I tried other localities.

"Have you ever been to the United States? Have you seen Hudson Bay? Have you even been to the southern tip of Greenland?"

Only Greenland struck a responsive chord.

"If that's as far as you've gone," I said, "you've much to see. The whole wide world is waiting."

"I have all the world I want," she said. "How could any world be more beautiful than this world?"

"There are mammoth cities. There are lighted streets. Swift traffic that rolls on wheels. Machines that carry voices and machines that throw postcard pictures on the wall—wonders that you've never dreamed of..."

Now Veeva was laughing at me. "I heard such talk before," she said. "So many of our enemies who come intending to spy upon us try to tell me these things. I am only amused. These are traps to lure me into the enemy's hands. But I am the queen, and I am too clever to be captured."

I gave back her laugh of ridicule. "And you accuse me of being suspicious!"

She started to draw her hand away. I held it tightly.

"Is there anything more you wish to say?" she asked.

"Only that I'm terribly in love with you," I said.

Her eyes widened, a high color rushed to her cheeks. But she made no reply. She drew her hand away—though I fancied that it lingered for an instant as I brushed my lips against it.

At once she was gone, and I was never so much alone.

CHAPTER SEVENTEEN
A Lord at Large

"YOU ought to be ashamed. You frightened her away," came a voice from my left.

"Steve Pound!" I gasped. "You're alive?"

"Righto. More than ever."

Steve's big blond countenance was before me, peering in through the carved stone gate. I tried to tell him he was a ghost but he denied it, reaching through to shake hands with me.

"You fellows didn't need to come," he said. "I was doing all right."

"Just what we figured," came Shorty's voice from my right. "It's no fair, Steve. I want that gal myself."

"I'm not talking about the girl," said Steve, and he sauntered on down the row of cells to greet Shorty and Professor Peterson.

Shorty must have been pretty badly stung over his recent talk with Veeva for he hopped on Steve with lively accusations.

"You've fixed things so she'll hardly talk with me," Shorty complained. "She laughs at everything I say."

"She brought you down here alive, didn't she?" said Steve. "You've got nothing to complain about. Did you see that row of ice domes along the valley trail?"

"From a distance," said Shorty.

"I got to see inside some of them," said Steve. "Men were frozen to death in those traps five years ago. I saw some of the remains. It's enough to make a fellow watch his step."

I heard Shorty gasp. "Who—who were they?"

"Members of Lord Lorruth's expedition—men that got too fresh and made a play for Veeva."

"Gosh!" Shorty groaned, and he expressed my sentiments precisely. "I better be careful how I talk."

"Any guy who feels like getting too friendly with the queen of these parts had better go out and take a look at those scattered skeletons."

I called Steve back to get the matter straight.

"It's tantamount to murder," I said. "I won't believe it of her. After all, what man can look at her without becoming infatuated? Is it any crime if a fellow's heart turns a flip-flop?"

"You'd better tie a rock to that heart of yours," said Steve. "But maybe you're right about her. These ice traps aren't straight murder. Anyhow she claims they *just happen*. When men start yelling at her, she can't help it if a dome of ice forms to hold 'em off."

"She can't?" I was highly dubious on this point, in spite of my anxiety to clear her character.

"But if those instantaneous igloos didn't happen," Steve went on, "she admits she'd have a lot more trouble keeping out of men's clutches. She's such a friendly thing, I figure this is nature's way of protecting her from the wrong men."

"I notice she hasn't flopped the ice over you," I observed, as the warmth of jealously rushed to my head. "I suppose you're immune. She doesn't even keep you locked up."

"I'm out on good behavior," Steve smiled. "That's what Lord Lorruth did for me. He warned me that if I attended strictly to business and didn't get any silly notions that the queen was interested in me—"

"*Who* warned you?" I gulped.

"Lord Lorruth. Here he comes now. Strictly a gentleman, that's his rule. I'll introduce you."

A TALL, bewhiskered, fur-clad gentleman was approaching. From his appearance, he might have been one of the natives. But his greetings were delivered with a mellow English accent.

"It's so kind of you men to make this trip on my behalf." He bowed graciously, casting his earnest gray eyes around the alcove. He had evidently stationed himself where Shorty and the professor could also see him. "I hope it will not inconvenience any of you if you are never allowed to return."

His manner was annoyingly mild and pleasant. It seemed to me that he might as easily have said, "We'll take pleasure in burning you at the stake. I hope you'll be happy about it."

Steve hastily supplemented this ominous remark.

"Lord Lorruth doesn't mean that just the way it sounds. He only means that now that we're all in his confidence, we couldn't be allowed to go back and tell his secrets."

"That's right," the tall elderly man smiled. "For my own part, staying right here is the easiest way."

I couldn't take all this in without considerable doubt. Lord Lorruth wasn't old. His shaggy whiskers and eyebrows were only slightly gray. Once out of this lost world, I thought, he would have thirty years of pleasant living before him.

"These friends of mine can be trusted," Steve was saying to Lord Lorruth. "And as soon as they settle down and prove they're not vicious agents of the...uh...enemy, Veeva will have them released from their cells."

"But they will still remain down in this world," Lord Lorruth added confidently.

"Of course—unless these people change their mind about the enemy."

"What's all this enemy talk?" I heard Professor Peterson demanding in an irate tone.

"It's a notion of theirs about an army of invaders," said Steve. "All five of us are a part of that army. As near as I can make out, they think there's a whole avalanche of warriors up on top waiting for a chance to crash the gates."

"Absurd!" I said. "No army would ever come up to this waste land."

"But these people never lack for evidence that their enemy is real," Lord Lorruth asserted. "The fact is, there have been many parties of visitors recently. To be sure, most of them, like twelve of my men, have been turned to ice before they ever start down the steps."

The professor was disturbed by this talk of other visitors recently. "What do you mean by...recently."

"In the last seven or eight centuries," said Lord Lorruth casually. "Recently enough to give the queen a smattering of modern languages—Latin. Scandinavian and English. Come along, Steve, if you want to help me with that packing."

"Then you've come to a decision," said Steve mysteriously. "All right, let's get busy."

CHAPTER EIGHTEEN
Firemakers' Fears

"PACKING? Packing? I snorted angrily. "What the devil did Lord Lorruth mean by that?"

"You explain it," said Shorty apathetically. "I'm busy pining over a lost love. But don't tell her, though, or I might end up in cold storage."

"Do you suppose," I went on, "that Lord Lorruth and Steve are going to get a tiger ride back to the *Aurora* and leave us here stranded?"

"You ought to know Steve better than that," the professor observed, making me half ashamed.

But I was in a cell and Steve was out, and I was a bit jealous and even a little wrought up.

"What if his talk about liking to stay here is only so much cake frosting to make us content with our fate?" I asked.

"I think this whole underground population is a bit on the crazy side" Shorty added.

"And I think you're both being a little absurd," the Professor decided.

He reminded us that these people were working with fine teamwork. There were no idlers—not even among the high-and-mighty Firemakers. There was a systematic division of labor. The artisans were highly skilled as evidenced by their careful gardening, their highly artistic metal works, and their immense engineering achievements—huge triangular doorways, roof supports, and ice dams.

THE Firemakers soon paid us a visit.

There were five of them. They were among the oldest of their subterranean culture. All of them had strong, fierce faces, coarse beards, deep-set eyes, powerful muscles. They would talk in low guttural voices as they discussed our fate.

One of them looked through the stone apertures at me.

"We know your new code. We can talk it as well as you. We have had it for two hundred darknesses."

By this I understood him to mean years. Their seasons came and went with the arctic days and nights. I discussed this code with him.

I tried to tell him he was only speaking my native tongue, the only one I had ever known. He considered my explanation subterfuge. He called the other four Firemakers over and repeated my excuse to them.

"But it's true," I declared. "I've come here with no knowledge of any enemy that might seek to harm you."

"That is exactly what I expected you to say," said the tallest of the Firemakers. "Don't strain yourselves in protesting your innocence."

Then I lost my temper. "I don't mind being insulted," I said. "But this is too much. I challenge you to prove that any man of us intends any harm. You don't believe me! All right. Go back and capture some of the others. Bring them here. Question them. They'll all tell you the same as I. We came here searching for one lost fur trader and his party."

The Firemakers exchanged doubting glances.

"How soon," I demanded, "are you going to let me out of here?"

"Let you out? That is a simple request."

ONE OF the Firemakers gestured to a group of small boys and together they tackled the huge slab of stone. Slowly it rolled to one side.

"Now," said the Firemaker, "you are out. What do you want to do about it?"

"I want to go home," I said, "and I can whip any man that tries to stand in my way."

"You're a very rough fellow," said the Firemaker. "We don't like to waste our hands on the grim business of fighting. But if you want to fight, take your anger out on these boys."

The group of lads, ranging from eight to twelve years of age, turned on me with their fierce little eyes and began doubling their fists.

"No," I protested. "Not these little fellows. But I'll take on the biggest of you."

The tallest of the Firemakers snapped his fingers and the seven or eight boys flew into me. I had a fight on my hands whether I liked it or not. I tried to wave them away. They tackled me around my ankles, flung themselves at my neck. They were all over me like a pack of wolves. I got a tight grip on the huskiest lad and began hurling him about, trying to knock off the others. But the lad was too strong.

They tightened their grips on my arms and legs and flung their weight at me until I swerved off balance. I went down under the dog-pile and they began pummeling me.

Even when I had a chance to strike a solid blow I couldn't do it. Not against these boys. This may have been the reason the tallest Firemaker suddenly called them off.

"I believe you now. You want to fight a man. That proves that you are no coward. But it proves too that our enemies are highly dangerous, if you are a fair example."

"Show me the way out of here," I demanded. "I'm leaving at once. Turn my pals loose—"

"Not so fast my friend," said the Firemaker. "If we let you go back, all our enemies will know where we are, how to find us, what our numbers are."

Then I saw the face of Professor Peterson gazing at me from his cell. He was shaking his head, warning me to quiet down. I walked back into my cell.

"All right," I said. "Roll the stone back in place."

The Firemaker laughed. "Very wise of you, my enemy. We will release you in due time, if your behavior is good."

TWO meals, a period of sleep, a few hours of silent waiting and wondering—then Veeva!

Veeva gave us the privilege of attending the council of the Firemakers.

The affair began with a feast. Veeva made it a lively, happy occasion, and whenever she laughed the Firemakers would have to laugh too—though some of them did a pretty sorry job of it.

Often Veeva's eyes would sparkle squarely at me, and once she quickly glanced at her hand as if she hadn't forgotten that I had tried to kiss it.

The Firemakers were full of noisy talk. Much of it was in our own language. Gradually we began to gather the threads of superstition that prevailed.

These people had believed for many, many years that some strange dangers awaited them. I tried to gauge the time, which their fear had encompassed, but this was impossible. When I talked in terms of Viking days, I learned that such times were recent to them.

These superstitions were a part of the fabric of their lives. It is hard to believe that people could believe in mortal fear year after year. Especially when no actual dangers beset them. But this fear had become engrained in their whole routine of life.

Where had it come from? How could it be dispelled?

Professor Peterson picked up a clue while listening to them. "What did you say," he asked, "about the coming of darkness?"

A Firemaker replied. "The darkness is a proof that our enemy is waiting," he said. "We must stay underground until all darkness is banished."

The professor gave me a funny look. This was incomprehensible. After all, there are no people in the world who are not accustomed to a certain regularity of darkness and light. Whether it is made of simple day and night, twelve hours each, as is the case on all continents toward the equator, or whether it is made of six months light or six months darkness as is the case on either pole, the inevitable succession of these phenomena is universal.

THE professor checked this point with a few telling questions and it became clear that they believed the coming of the arctic night was in itself a proof that the enemies were still at hand waiting to demolish them.

Peterson whispered to me, "Do you suppose there are any books or records in this world? Can we trace it down, Jim? This freak notion had to have had a beginning. They didn't make it up out of thin air."

"It's amazing," I said reflectively. "These people seem to have lived here for centuries."

Now it came our time to offer our bows of obeisance, and I felt extremely awkward.

Peterson set the pace by bowing to the floor. He actually placed his face against the surface of stone. There he waited until Veeva sang her little song with the jumbled words.

The wholehearted manner in which he carried out his gesture of respect was a lesson to me. I felt that Shorty and I were a pair of sentimental boobs, hopelessly in love, but missing all the little things that really counted with a queen.

But Professor Peterson had been a student; he knew the ways of many races and tribes, and his knowledge was serving him in good stead.

Now Veeva invited us to speak our piece to the Firemakers if there was anything we wanted to say. Peterson responded with the utmost of suavity.

"I'm pleased with this hospitality. I bring you greetings from the world above. With your permission I would like to convey our greetings *directly to the King himself.*"

This speech pleased the Firemakers, and the tallest of them arose to make a dignified response.

"After the feast is finished," he said, "you will be conducted into the presence of the King. In fact, the King will desire to pronounce his judgment upon the 'fates' of the three of you."

This ominous forecast gave my heart a sudden jump. I was worried that for once Professor Peterson had overdone it. If he hadn't requested an audience with the king, we might have been placed back in our cells long enough to figure out a way of escape from our ice-bound prison. But Peterson, it seemed to me, wanted his potential execution pronounced sooner rather than later, and so we were off to see the king.

CHAPTER NINETEEN
A Rebel Returns

OUR procession was interrupted near a stairway by an excited clamor of voices.

A swarm of boys came down, rolling, tumbling, fighting, yelling. They had a prisoner—Gandl.

They forced him across the room toward us. Some guards shouted orders, and it was apparent that the Firemakers were amazed. Our reception had been mild compared to this.

Gandl broke away. The boys chased after him. They caught him and dragged him down. They were savage little demons and they fought like a pack of wolves.

Gandl, for all his strength, was no match for them.

I didn't know what it was all about but I couldn't stand to see Gandl being whipped by boys. When the fight tumbled around in our direction I couldn't restrain myself. I jumped right into the fray and started jerking the boys off Gandl's back. There were twenty or more of them. It was a regular free-for-all. Peterson and Shorty got into it, too. I heard Shorty yell for help and discovered that he was being tossed about by one small group of savages who seemed on the verge of tearing him apart.

The guards pitched in too before the fight was over. They had stone weapons—long tomahawk affairs with bone handles and stone mallets. It would have been unwise to resist.

Gandl had a tough fighting face, but there was always that mysterious something in his eyes, keen and intelligent. They dragged him to a table and there we all gathered around for the strangest conference I have ever attended.

At last we discovered what Gandl's place was in this entire affair...

He was a runaway.

Yes, Gandl the stowaway was actually a member of this forgotten race. He was a rebel, a fighter, and a doubter. In every way he was a thorn in the flesh of the Firemakers and their people.

Their questions to him brought out his story of his numerous runaway experiences. He had left for the first time five years before. That was after he had encountered Lord Lorruth. Gandl's passion for exploring the outside world had been too great; he had wandered southward.

From Greenland he had found a passage to the United States, and now, after all these years of roaming around the world, he had returned to his native land of ice.

But as we sailors knew, he had not walked in expecting a glorious welcome. He had hung back to hide, to watch and listen from a distance, realizing it would be unsafe to show his face, for he had violated the traditions of loyalty and had deserted an important position.

This came out in our present conference. One of the Firemakers addressed him as "Gandl, the King's Advisor." But the tallest Firemaker sharply canceled the title.

"Gandl is no longer the King's Advisor. He has renounced his right to that title."

"I had a more important service to perform," said Gandl.

"No service," said the Firemaker, "could be any more important than being the Advisor to the King. You have betrayed our whole nation. You have brought shame upon us by doubting our age-old beliefs."

"I not only doubt them," said Gandl stoutly, "but I bring back proofs that they are false."

This blasphemy so horrified the Firemakers and various officers that sat with us, I thought they might execute Gandl on the spot. I looked to Veeva, but apparently it was not her turn to speak. She tossed her head and walked away, leaving the situation in the hands of these stony elders.

FOR a minute the only words were the fearful whispers which passed among the members of the council. The tallest Firemaker glared at Gandl and tried to look him down. The tall gaunt man's fingers were trembling. His lips were white. With an attitude of tremendous power, he placed his great arms at the side of the table and shouted.

"Gandl I defy you to say one more word that would weaken our state against the enemies. Have they converted you? Have *they* filled your blood with poison? Have *they* shouted threats in your ears that you should come back to sell us into their hands?"

"There is no enemy," Gandl retorted in a voice as cold as ice. He leaned across the table to return the Firemaker's fierce stare. He beat his fists. He shouted, "You're fools, living down here in this frozen hell. You don't know what world lies beyond because you're afraid. There is *no* enemy! There has been no enemy for countless centuries."

"It's a lie!" the tall Firemaker screamed.

"It's the truth." Gandl's dark eyes blazed hot fire. "I challenge you to follow me, to go over the path where I have gone, to see the free people—"

The tall Firemaker couldn't stand it. In one furious leap he bounded to the stone table. A second leap and he threw the whole of his weight against Gandl. The two of them went rolling on the floor, snarling like a pair of bloodthirsty beasts. They tore at each other's throats. They cursed and snarled and fought with unabated fury. The tall Firemaker's fingernails slashed long red lines down Gandl's arm.

The other Firemakers gathered in upon them closely, eagerly. They were sure this would be the end of Gandl. But suddenly a shrill cry came from the lips of Veeva.

"Gee-olo-fro-goff!"

It was a language that I didn't understand—but a language so forceful that her utterance sent chills leaping through my spine.

Everyone turned. Veeva, the Queen, was standing beside her polar tiger. The big jaws of the beast were wide open, the teeth gleaming. Instantly the conflict came to a stop.

The tall Firemaker drew himself up to full height and began to back away. The other Firemakers grouped around him and the boy servants lined up on either side of them.

The action had stopped, but not the emotional tension. We were lined up now like two armies. The Firemakers were fighting to hang on to their age-old traditions but Gandl had come home filled with new knowledge. His very eyes blazed with "treason."

This was all wrong—this life of theirs—and Gandl had come to tell them so. Naturally the professor and Shorty and I were with him one hundred per cent. I only wish that Steve and Lord Lorruth had been with us—but they had evidently gone their own way hours before.

Here between the two warring camps stood Veeva herself, with one arm around the throat of the ferocious white beast. She was the balance of power. If she favored one side more than the other she concealed it. And now, as so often before, she applied her most potent weapon. She laughed.

NO one else could laugh. The rest of us were too weak, too much partisans of this struggle. Her laughter was her power and she made us feel ridiculous.

Then suddenly she whipped out a brisk speech, aimed squarely at the Firemakers.

"You clumsy fools. Are you trying to amuse me with your wrestling match?" She ruffled the tiger's ears. "On my left I have my loyal white servant, on my right I have my sword. *I promise death to the first man who threatens Gandl without my permission.*"

No one was quicker to pretend recovery than the tall Firemaker. He and the other dignitaries bowed low and assured the queen that they were her most humble and loyal of servants. What would she command?

"Sit down. Place yourselves at the table and listen to me."

They obeyed.

She told them that they must listen to Gandl's words. But they would not have the *privilege* of deciding his fate until the King himself had been consulted.

The tall Firemaker answered with a slight tone of sarcasm.

"Do you intend to wait until the King has awakened?"

"You know the answer to that," said Veeva sharply. "When have we ever waited for the King to awaken before we consult him on matters of importance?"

"But you know the law. Only the King's Advisor can consult him through a mingling of their dreams."

There was considerable discussion about this point. I gathered that the King had been sleeping for a very long time. It seemed, however, that these people believed his opinions could be learned by his Advisor, even though both were sleeping. That is, the King's Advisor held his special office by virtue of being able to enter into the King's own dreams. Then, upon awakening the Advisor could tell the Firemakers what the sleeping King wished.

"But how can we enter into his dream when we have no loyal Advisor?" the Firemakers protested. "Gandl has turned traitor. He is no longer qualified to receive the King's dreams."

But Veeva quickly topped this argument. "Whether he is a traitor or not is for the King to decide. Have you Firemakers lost your wits? Cannot you still whisper your questions to the King as you have always done?"

Slowly, perhaps even begrudgingly, the Firemakers nodded in the affirmative. This was their one special power.

"Very well," said Veeva. "You will hold a ceremony of whispers at once. You will inform the King that we are questioning the loyalty of his Advisor."

"And how will we know his answer?"

"You will tell him," said Veeva, "that Gandl is ready to lie down on the stone near his bed, to dream with him. If Gandl is no longer loyal, the King is to strike him dead."

CHAPTER TWENTY
The King's Prolonged Nap

BEFORE the Firemakers could recover their tongues, Veeva pressed on with her swift challenge.

"Do you understand me?" she snapped. "If the King does not strike Gandl dead that will prove his loyalty. Accordingly we may believe the dream which Gandl receives."

I saw a faint smile on Professor Peterson's lips. It was indeed a most intriguing plan. I suspected that Veeva realized her stroke of cleverness.

I assumed all this talk of conversing within dreams was a flight of fancy. But when I stopped to consider the strange things that had already occurred in the recent past, I realized I dare not be too skeptical. Perhaps this agreement would spell tragedy for Gandl!

Might the King actually have the power to deal death even while he was sleeping? So far as I knew he might.

We were taken back to our cells. There was a long period of waiting. We saw only the guards for many hours. Work had ceased. The chattering boys had taken themselves to their separate homes, which consisted of branches of the cavern off the main stream.

Professor Peterson was highly excited. He kept talking in terms of faraway races and cultures. He was very curious about these superstitions, and wondered if they, like many of the artifacts of this region, were related to those of the early European cavemen.

He compared their tools, their weapons, and their art, and declared these people must have a definite kinship with the Cro-Magnon cultures of long ago.

But I was beginning to grow impatient with Peterson's ramblings. I wanted to get out. I felt sure that Steve had escaped, or soon would.

But could I get Professor Peterson to help us lay a plan for escape? It seemed unlikely at the moment. One would have thought he was a treasure hunter who had already come into his cave full of precious gems from the way he was talking.

"Those dots along the wall—did you notice them, Jim?" he asked.

"Fancy ornaments, all right," I said, "but how does that help us get out of here?"

"Those dots came to an end right there in the middle of the Red Room," Shorty recalled.

"But why should they?" the professor asked. "Why didn't the artist carry them on along the whole wall? There must be some reason. And their stone dishes. Have you studied them carefully, Jim? I never saw any like them outside a museum. Once when I was in Heidelberg looking over the old Cro-Magnon relics—"

Shorty broke in with a more serious topic. "This business of a King who doesn't do anything but sleep—I don't get it. What makes him sleep so much?"

"I don't know," said Peterson. "That's another thing I'd like to find out before we leave."

"What gets me," said Shorty, "is that Veeva is married to such a lazy goof. You'd think a girl like her wouldn't stand for it."

Peterson chuckled at this. "I suppose I could agree with you on that point," he answered.

SHORTY continued, "Just think of it. Here she's been all gone all these weeks and when she comes back and they have a celebration for her and everything, what does the King do? He keeps right on sleeping."

The professor said, "If you boys weren't in such a hurry to get away, we might pick up some of the most colorful ethnological data ever discovered. Don't you see what we have here—a rich vein of primitive culture. Somehow it has escaped the erosions of time. The modern age hasn't touched it. It's pure and unadulterated and beautiful in its simplicity. It may hold for science the answer to thousands of mysteries."

Shortly blinked. "Could you say that over?"

"I mean," said Peterson, "that if we learned about these ceremonies we might go back to the big universities of Europe and America. They would like to know about these things. This ritual of dreams is the most innocent artifice I've ever run across."

"The thing that's got me going round and round," I said, "is their talk about *time*. You'd think that they'd lived here for ages."

"Perhaps they have."

"But *these* folks haven't. You know this girl Veeva can't be more than twenty or twenty-two years old."

"My guess is eighteen," said Shorty.

"Anyway," I persisted, "she talks like she's lived a thousand years."

There was a long silence.

"I wonder where Steve and Lord Lorruth are?" Shorty murmured drowsily.

"Under a mound of ice somewhere, frozen to death," I offered out of a growing mental gloom.

"I wonder if Lady Lucille is plumb crazy for keeps."

"She's probably chasing the Frabbel brothers with a knife."

"It'd serve 'em right," Shorty grunted. "I wonder... I wonder if the King and Veeva were happy together before he went to sleep..."

"It's a curious pattern," Professor Peterson resumed presently, as if he had wakened up the middle of a half completed lecture, "but as you gentlemen doubtless know, primitive people are the most frightened people in the world. They live by their fears. They build up their whole religion over some peculiar obsession. The slightest incident may be magnified into a powerful taboo. And it's happened here undoubtedly."

"You mean their fear of *the enemy?*" I asked.

"That's it," said Peterson. "Somehow they have associated the six month darkness with the approaching of dangers. It probably started ages ago, and now look at the silly belief they are nurturing. Each time the year's sunlight disappears they insist that the enemy is again upon them. They are waiting for the time that a permanent light will come."

A GUARD, followed by a squad of boys, came trudging toward our alcove.

"Prisoners, where are you? Prisoners, where are you?" The guard went over his little singsong rhythm. "Come out. Veeva wants to see you immediately. Follow me."

His squad opened our doors, and he turned and walked off, confident that we would follow him. We did.

The Queen herself rode across the vast Red Room floor to meet us.

"Come, follow me. I promised that you would meet the King."

"Is he awake?" Shorty blurted anxiously.

The girl laughed. "We can't wait for that. I've been waiting for thousands of years for him to awaken."

"Thousands?" the professor asked gravely.

"Thousands," said Veeva.

Shorty jumped at the chance to pursue this topic.

"Thousands of years! Did he tell you it would be like that, or did you just figure he was droppin' down fer an afternoon nap?"

"I've never talked with him," the girl said.

"Never?" I gasped. "But at the time you married him you must have at least said 'I do' or something."

Veeva smiled at me and gave a funny little toss of her head as if these matters didn't concern her too much.

"I've no particular recollection of getting married to him. I only know that his sleep began before the ceremony, and he's never been awake since."

THE passage from the Red Room led into a narrow winding tunnel. Soon we were ascending steps that were hewn out of the brightest pink stone. The walls, too, were a luminous pink. The color lent a magic to this winding stairway.

When we reached the top of the ascent, we seemed to be in complete darkness. Then our eyes adjusted, and the scene became half-visible. We were in a round blue-walled chamber, as spherical as if it had been cut with a diamond point.

Thin lines of deep blue light encircled us like windings of luminous blue wire. The room was about fifty-five feet wide. The ceiling was lost in the steamy blue darkness. A few stone benches could be seen, lined around the circular wall.

We spoke in whispers. Every breath, every whisper, every footstep echoed round and round.

"The Firemakers are here," said Veeva. "They are watching Gandl."

"Is he sleeping?" Shorty asked.

"That's all he does. It is such a sleep that you will think him dead," said Veeva. "But he is the King."

To her, that explained everything.

"How do you know that the Firemakers haven't killed him?"

Shorty's suggestion was shocking to Veeva. She was quick with a confident answer—an answer that was packed with superstition. "They wouldn't dare. If they thought of such a thing, the King himself would strike them dead. He sleeps with a jeweled dagger at his side."

"I see," said Professor Peterson, choosing to stifle any further questions from Shorty. When the professor found a guarded moment he whispered a bit of advice to us. "Don't say things that would suggest any doubt to Veeva's faith in the King."

"Only Gandl has cut through this maze of blind faith," Peterson warned us. "The girl is as saturated with it as the Firemakers themselves."

We sat on the stone benches, staring at the deep gloom in the center of the room. We were in the King's presence now.

The light was dim, but Veeva assured us he was there on a coffin-shaped resting-place. She led us to the middle of the room where the light seemed somewhat better

The unbelievable was at hand. There lay Gandl on a simple slab of stone. That was his bed, right beside the King's. It was a full step lower and it made me wonder whether a King's dreams flowed downhill.

Now I could make out the figure of the King, a long slender form of darkness upon the highly ornamented bed of stone.

The light was too dim for me to be sure Gandl was breathing. He was as still as death. My heart skipped a beat. Could it be that the sleeping King had already acted?

But how could he? It was silly for me to fall into the spell of these ignorant superstitions. The power of any King, sleeping or awake, lies in the belief of his people in him.

We moved from Gandl to the more ornamental bed. The moment of meeting was at hand.

Veeva stood before us. Her manner was reverent. She was motioning us to look down upon this figure. This undoubtedly was the only person in the world to whom she was subject.

Then we gazed down at the shadows. I could make out a little dagger, bright with jewels, lying at the King's side. But the King was nothing more nor less than an old gray skeleton, crumbling in decay.

FOR a few minutes I did not realize what perils were impending. It was all silence that prevailed in this chilled room of the cave. It was a frightening silence.

The King had lain there for thousands of years, a heap of dry bones. And yet, by the strange miracle of iron-bound tradition, he was the ruler of this lost civilization. And now once more he was about to exert his will.

The Firemakers sat rigidly, their cruel eyes burning fiercely through the darkness. They were like statues, but one could not easily forget that they were present. Peterson, Shorty and I retired to the farther end of the rounded room. I had edged around until the sight of Gandl came clearly. A dim light glinted off his profile, and there was a slow rhythmic breathing evident in the turning of reflected light over the iron muscles of his chest.

Shorty whispered to me, "How in hell can the King kill him?"

"The King *can't.*"

The round walls of the room echoed our whispers, and we dared say no more. But suddenly the whole situation came clear to me. I saw the ritual for what it was—gross superstition. And to think I had almost fallen for it!

Yes, the Firemakers had everything their way. All they needed to do was to destroy Gandl and their authority would remain unchallenged. They *would* destroy Gandl and somehow make the people believe the King had done it.

A sound of footsteps intruded. The boys were coming. Their chattering voices hushed as they approached the door of the King's room. I saw the tallest Firemaker gesture to his fellows to remain seated. Then he crossed to the entrance.

"What do you want?"

There was a low jumble of conversation in the language I could not understand. The tall Firemaker appeared to be relieved. He turned to his fellows.

"The ice roof is crumbling three rooms beyond the red corridor. Go! All help is needed." He turned to us. "You, too. Your help is needed at once. Follow the boys."

Terrifying chills raced through my spine. Nothing had frightened me more during our descent than the thought of being buried alive under a collapse of the ice. I knew the ceilings could not be stable when there were such frequent evidences of breaks and faults. And so for an instant I was taken in. We all moved toward the door—all except the tall Firemaker, who sauntered back, intent on remaining here.

I acted on impulse. I rolled under a low shelf of rock that had been left for a bench. Here the darkness was complete. The Firemaker could not see me.

He paced uneasily until the voices of the retreating party faded away. Finally he sat down on the stone bench. Again everything was deathly silent.

I hardly dared breathe. Among these round walls the slightest sound was dreadfully magnified. But I had a terrifying curiosity that made me want to crawl the length of this hiding place to make sure no one else was with me. A foolish thought. I had seen everyone go. There were only the four of us now—the tall Firemaker, and Gandl asleep, the dead King, and myself.

Was Gandl asleep?

The tall Firemaker seemed to be pondering that question, too. He must have doubts or he would have murdered Gandl on the spot. Now he sauntered to the doorway and I could hear his footsteps retreating down the hall.

This was perfect. It gave me a chance to know whether Gandl was asleep or only pretending. I made the most of my opportunity; I crawled out of my shadowy hiding-place and crept over to Gandl's side.

"Listen, Gandl. It's me, Jim McClurg. I'm here watching you. There's no one on guard now except the tall Firemaker. Do you hear me?"

Gandl made no response other than a slight change in the rhythm of his breathing.

"I have something to say to you," I persisted. "You know their proposition. The King is supposed to whisper his will to you. But you know he can't do that. It's impossible. Do you hear me?"

CHAPTER TWENTY-ONE
Gandl Hears the King

GANDL breathed drowsily. "Go ahead. I'm listening. Are you the King?"

"It's me, Jim McClurg. Are you going to lie here and let them kill you?"

Such a heaviness of sleep was upon him that he must have been having nightmares. From his mumbling I gathered that he thought I was the King and that he welcomed my whisper.

"They are going to kill me if I don't get your message. They think you won't speak to me because I am a rebel."

That was my cue. I could not pass it by.

I whispered in a heavy authoritative accent that I thought a king might use:

"I am the King. I am talking with you, Gandl. Have you ever heard me before?"

"No, never. I have only pretended. This is the first time your voice has reached me. I never believed in you. I thought you were nothing but Death."

"But you do hear me now, and I have many things to say to you."

"I'm listening."

"First of all, you were right to leave this place and visit the lands beyond. Now that you have come back, you must tell these people what you have seen. There are no enemies abroad."

Gandl murmured happily, "No enemy. That's what I told them. I did not find anyone in the outside world who was not a friend." Then his tone changed. "But you are asleep, and if there are no enemies, why don't you awaken?"

This question stumped me. I had run into a trap of my own making, but I took a long chance.

"I can't awaken. I am dead. Whether enemies come or go, I shall always remain in a state of death. But you, Gandl, you must lead the people out of their ignorance."

"Have I the power? The Firemakers would not let me——"

"You must over-rule them," I commanded.

"Does Veeva know that you are dead?"

"If you tell her that I have come to you in this dream, giving you my last message, she will believe."

"I will tell her," said Gandl, "but will she not be heartbroken?"

My heart almost stopped beating as I realized what power lay in my hands at this moment. But I had already plunged, and if my trick failed, I would have earned death already. So I replied to Gandl with the bold answer that inflamed my mind.

"You must tell her that it is time for her to choose a new king."

"A new king...a new king..."

Gandl drifted back into the deep mists of sleep

I started to crawl back to the side of the room, but something stopped me. Echoing footsteps; the Firemaker was returning. I hastily hid myself under Gandl's low bed beside the resting-place of the King. For many minutes I watched the sandaled feet of the tall Firemaker as he walked around.

"Sleeping well, my friend?" the Firemaker whispered. Gandl made no response.

"The ice is falling in some of the rooms beyond. There is danger."

This suggestion apparently made no impression on the sleeping rebel. But I knew that the Firemaker was testing to make sure that his victim was sound asleep.

The sandaled feet came near to the stone bed right before my eyes. I knew that the Firemaker was hovering over Gandl now.

Then I heard a metallic scraping over the King's resting-place. That was the little jeweled dagger. The Firemaker had picked it up. Now he was taking a stance, his feet wide apart. The moment was at hand.

I STRUCK with all my force. My right arm swung like a mallet against the Firemaker's left ankle. With a flash of light, a silver sandal swept upward and the tall man went down. His metal bracelets clanked against the floor.

I rolled out from under the stone. My eyes were sharp for signs of the jeweled dagger, and my hands groped. But my only advantage was another strike at his ankles, and for the second time I hurled him off balance.

Then I saw that the weapon of death was still in his hand. He was bounding up, coming at me. In the dimness he was but three spots of light—a pair of fiery eyes and the gleaming blade.

I was on my feet now, and instantly I raced away to the far side of the elevated resting-place of the King.

In doing so I left Gandl unprotected, and the poor fellow was still sleeping. How fatigued he must have been from his journey over the ice wilderness, or was he perhaps sleeping into death? Once more the grip of this underworld magic was upon him. Strange, that such thoughts could paralyze me in the brief seconds that held the fate of Veeva and her people in the balance.

Above all, Gandl must not be killed. For that would restore the Firemakers to power and exalt them and magnify their glory for generations to come.

The Firemaker glided to the edge of Gandl's stone bed, like a bird about to take flight. He was plunging over the top to me. Gandl and the King were merely his stepping-stones. Veeva should have seen that!

With upraised arm he plunged down at me. I flung myself at his feet once more, and he went sprawling across the floor. To my horror, some of the bones from the dusty old skeleton fell with him, for he had tripped over the King in crossing. As he lay there, momentarily stunned by his fall, I could see the decaying bones of the King's hand lying across his metal sandal. Somehow, that glimpse struck home. Even as I rushed forward, impelled to capture the dagger, I paused long enough to fling a hand at that bit of skeleton. It scooted under the stone bed.

That was a costly moment. I might have had my hands on the dagger, but the tall Firemaker was coming back into action in a flash. He rolled away from me and bounded up on his feet. I think I got in three or four blows over his head and back before he could wheel on me.

Instantly the chase was on again, and I was retreating. The room fairly roared with the noise of battle. It was enough to wake the King from the dead. How many times we stumbled around the regal resting-place, I do not know.

My moments were numbered. Once the blade ripped down across the back of my hand. My feet were like lead, it seemed, and my breath was gone. I seemed to be guiding myself more by sound than sight, keeping out of range of the shadowy form, scowling and panting and growling threats in weird words that I could not understand.

Then I picked up the only weapon I could lay my hands on—a bone from the resting-place of the King. I hurled a thighbone full into the Firemaker's face. For an instant he staggered, then I was upon him, clutching the gaunt wrist, which was frozen upon the dagger. We struggled back and forth in a deadlock. Once the tip of the blade cut the side of my neck. Until that moment I had hoped to knock out my enemy somehow, without doing him mortal injury. But it was kill or be killed.

Summoning all my strength, I forced him over the King's resting-place. He tripped, and his long, shadowy body fell. His elbow was under him as he went down, and the dagger plunged up through his chest.

CHAPTER TWENTY-TWO
Gandl's Farewell to the King

HE was quiet. I shrank back to the wall, rubbing my hands, terrified over the hideous thing I had done.

I waited. There were no further sounds of breathing. Those little murmurings came from Gandl, I wonder what weird nightmares he had endured during his battle.

I could hear his voice becoming distinct.

"I will tell them," he said, "that you are dead. Veeva must choose another king. That's what I will tell them."

His words brought me to my senses. There was no time to lose. Even now I could hear a growing clamor of voices from a distance. The other Firemakers were returning. Again I whispered:

"You are right, Gandl, I, the King, am at last dead. But I must whisper to you one more secret. There was one Firemaker who would not believe what you are about to tell them. And so, as my last act, I have killed him. You must tell the others I have done this, and they will believe."

I hastily dragged the body of the tall Firemaker to the side of the room where he had previously stationed himself. His fur clothing had absorbed a part of his blood, so that no trail was left.

I returned to the King's resting-place and recovered the skeletal hand. It was almost complete. One of the bones of the lower arm was attached, part of the little finger was missing. I closed this cluster of bones around the handle of the dagger, which still hung in the dead Firemaker's chest.

By the time the party returned the scene was in order. I was hidden. I held my breath and listened.

Veeva and the most loyal of her Firemakers were the first to arrive. They paused in the doorway. Gandl was mumbling.

"He is still asleep," Veeva said.

"Can you see him?"

"Our eyes will adjust to the light in a moment," said the friendly Firemaker. "Come—I will lead you to him. He is talking in his sleep."

The low mumbling went on for several minutes, and I could hear Veeva whispering to her companion as they tried to make out what Gandl was saying.

"Yes, I have heard your message," Gandl said. "Are you gone now...? Are you gone...? Come back, O King, and say these words to them. I am afraid they won't believe me. They call me a rebel... What, you assure me that they will believe?"

Other Firemakers appeared at the doorway and waited there, listening to this weird, one-sided communication. Veeva whispered to them to stay back.

"He is talking with the King. He is receiving some very strange message. He thinks we will not believe him because he is a rebel."

The friendly Firemaker added in an impressive voice, "Of course we will believe him. We have no other choice. Listen! I can almost hear the King whispering to him myself."

"Yes, O King!" Gandl murmured softly. "I will tell them that you have performed your last acts of service... You have killed a Firemaker who would have refused to believe... Yes, I understand. Your service is done. You are destroying yourself... Farewell, O King!"

I WAITED until the murdered body was discovered, to make sure the circumstantial evidence was accepted. This, I knew, would be the supreme test of the Firemakers' faith in their own superstitions.

They were horrified, shocked, but unsuspecting.

I was satisfied. The evidence was scanty, and details couldn't be observed under the dim light. But Gandl, still lost in his dreamy trance, was behaving so perfectly that the observers were forced to listen to him. They were convinced that he was echoing the words of the King.

But now the King was only a scattered pile of bones.

No wonder, then, that Gandl kept calling for the King to come back and tell him more.

The alarming presence of the murdered Firemaker served to reinforce their superstitions rather than shake them.

"That's what comes of doubting," whispered the friendliest of the Firemakers, and the others listened to him respectfully. "This man, our Firemaker brother, remained here intending to supervise the conference of dreams. His doubt of Gandl, the Rebel, was likewise a doubt of the King. In fact, he hoped to discredit Gandl's report. And so—*the King has spoken with the dagger.*"

There were murmurs of approval. A spell of awe held the group in a frigid grip. Shaky faiths became solid on the spot.

And there I had my answer. Were the Firemakers sincere in their belief that this heap of dry bones held power over life and death? Indeed they were, if the King was in a mood to stab them for insincerity.

The bony hand still clung to the dagger, and several Firemakers kept watching for fear it might move.

Gradually these listeners pieced together the low mumblings of Gandl, and they realized what a tremendous event had taken place. The King had performed his last official act and had gone into a final death voluntarily.

CHAPTER TWENTY-THREE

The Queen Is Interrupted

"OUR poor bereaved Queen!" the Firemakers began to whisper. "How can she endure this great sorrow?"

That was when I discreetly removed myself from the scene. I was a trembling mass of nerves, with just enough self-control to keep myself hidden. I couldn't stand to hear any more. I had bet on superstition and won. I had murdered and got away with it. But when these men began overflowing with condolences for Veeva because a rattley old skeleton had been knocked to pieces—when they referred to it as her dear husband—well, it was all I could do to hold back an outburst of wild laughter.

I slipped along through the dark corridors and hid myself wherever there was danger of meeting a group of boys or a stray workman. For once the thought of being locked securely in a cell was very appealing.

I found an icy spring of water back in a remote branch of the cavern, and there I bathed my wounds. My neck had scarcely bled, but I had gone to no end of trouble to avoid leaving blood tracks from my ripped hand.

I remained in hiding, and whiled the hours away in rest and troubled dreams. All the literary gems I had ever read about murder marched through my mind in a gruesome procession.

Four errand boys discovered me, finally, and demanded to know what I was doing here. I convinced them that I had lost my way.

"We carry words from your friend," one of them said.

Out of their broken English I was made to understand that Steve and Lord Lorruth—the latter in disguise—had made the perilous trip out over the ice with a party of workers—"To take big furs to some woman on ship. Much mad woman."

"How much mad?" I asked.

"Big much mad. Want more big furs."

"Did Steve and Lord Lorruth tell her they would bring her some more?"

"Tell her nothing. Lay furs on ice near ship. Hurry back. Woman yell at them, mad like falling stones."

"Then Steve and Lord Lorruth came back here?" I asked.

"Yes. Now in big Red Room to hear Queen make speech."

There were several thousand persons on hand, I found, listening to the pronouncements of Veeva the Queen. By borrowing a suit of furs from the unoccupied shelter of some native, I was able to edge my way into the vast assembly without attracting any attention whatsoever.

Who would she choose for her new King? The girl was speaking now.

I MELTED away at the sound of her voice. What magical beauty was hers! She was mounting a stairway that had been hewn in the side of the wall, and the glow of colored light sifted over her lovely face and form.

Her white Tiger was with her. It fidgeted nervously, obviously bothered by the size of the crowd; but whenever she paused to speak, it would stand motionless, attentive.

The stairs led to a little balcony carved in the wall. Here, thirty feet above the crowd, Veeva and the white tiger were highlighted by a glow of pink light from the surrounding wall.

My worshipful trance was interrupted by a low-whispered conversation of a group of natives close at hand. One of the Firemakers was among them.

"The falling ice from three rooms beyond? No, it was nothing serious," he assured them. "I regret that I left the King's chamber to investigate it."

"But some are saying that more breaks are coming in a straight path toward this hall."

"We've been patching breaks for thousands of years," said the Firemaker. "Any King worthy of our beautiful queen will protect us."

The whispered talk was lost to me, for I was crowding forward to be nearer Veeva.

The quickening of my heart was like a restless sea. As I crowded forward I wondered whether Steve and the rest of the party were searching for me. Now that the furs had been recovered for Lady Lucille, would she not demand that we set sail for home the minute the winter ice began to break?

Undoubtedly Steve and Lord Lorruth had returned only to round up Peterson, Shorty, and me. But I wasn't exactly ready to go. Not just yet. My eyes were feasting on the most gorgeous human being I ever hoped to see, and a new fire was leaping within me.

Veeva's words flowed on like music. Most of the talk I couldn't understand. But the crowd was liking it, and their admiration for such a queen was wonderful to see.

She looked down at me and for an instant her words stopped, and she smiled faintly. The white tiger leaped up to place his forepaws on the rail. Veeva recovered her broken sentence and went on. The animal relaxed.

In that moment I was saying to myself, "Before I leave this place I'm going to tell her. She may laugh, she may pity me, she may have me imprisoned in ice, but before she has time to think about that new King, I'll have her know I'm desperately in love—"

My thoughts broke off, for my eyes chanced to fall upon a group of dignitaries. There was Gandl among them, looking squarely at me. He may have read my thoughts. Or he may have sensed, within me, that someone's destiny was in the balance.

At any rate I guessed, in that instant, who the next King would be. I realized that the only thing that had stood between Veeva and Gandl in the past was the trifling difference between faith and skepticism.

Now, at last, Gandl might enjoy the full favor of these people, even though he was a rebel. For had the old King not done a murder in his behalf? They thought so.

Now Veeva repeated an announcement in English, and I caught my breath.

"When I speak to you again from these stairs, I will tell you who is to be the new King. But I cannot tell you now— for I do not know."

She concluded with a merry laugh, and the crowd laughed with her.

It was a welcome note of gaiety, the first that I had heard for many hours. But it was cut short.

CHAPTER TWENTY-FOUR
The Queen Recalls

A HALF-TON slab of ice, bulging from a crack in the vertical wall, dropped. The crowd surged back as the ice struck with a crash and a spray of splinters.

There was a momentary vibration underfoot. The earth was trembling. A spider-web of cracks appeared in the wall. Suddenly a section of the narrow stone stairs was falling.

Screams rang above the rumble of falling stones. The crowd became a flowing tide racing out of the path of danger.

But there was no general avalanche. The massive luminous walls defied the shudder. Only the fragile structures felt the shock—the wall ornaments, the carved shelves, the arcades and the ceremonial stairs. And there was Veeva—

"Kroff! Kroff!" The cry rang through the big room. It was the native word for "Jump!"

Just as the upper-stairs and tiny balcony rattled and cracked and broke loose, Veeva acted.

She leaped to the back of Whitey and slapped him on the neck. He pushed off with his paws and flew for the floor.

In that split second I saw a stray rock bounce from the wall and strike Veeva on the side of the head. The crowd screamed. They couldn't understand it—Veeva the Queen falling from her mount in midair.

The tiger, I was later told, made a most graceful landing, and whirled about in surprise to see what had happened to its rider. But I did not see. I was one of the few persons close enough to help break Veeva's fall. I rushed into the path of her descent with outstretched arms. We fell to the floor in a heap.

I was slow regaining my feet. Veeva was now in my arms. Declining help from others, I carried her to the nearby station of a native physician. I kept murmuring soft words to her and even kissed the side of her cheek.

As we entered the medical station, which was a sizable, ornate structure, much of the crowd followed and kept swarming around, directing me to an elegant room with luminous copper-colored walls. Everyone was clamoring to know whether Veeva was all right. Her eyes were only half-open, and her long fine hair floated against my bare shoulder. She seemed to be telling the crowd that everything was all right by waving her hand weakly.

Hours later it was a quiet little party that surrounded the Queen of the Ice, lying regally on the couch.

Back in the corner of the elegantly carved room was Whitey, ever silent, ever attentive. If Shorty could have been only half as mannerly! He was forever wanting to talk when I was already speaking.

But the substance of that memorable conversation was between Professor Peterson and Veeva.

Veeva was still in a sort of stupor from the blow on her head. But she was talking—talking lucidly of many things.

"I'll want some of you to bear witness to these words," Professor Peterson whispered to us. "We're hearing some frank conversation at last. I doubt she would ever speak so freely if she weren't slightly out of her head."

GANDL'S eyes shone as he listened to these secret revelations. Part of the time Lord Lorruth and Steve Pound were present. And Shorty and I never missed a word.

"If you are still grieving over the loss of the King," said Professor Peterson to the girl, "I hope you will accept our sympathy."

"Most of all I am worried," said Veeva, "about the woman on the ship. I have feelings that she means to harm me... But I am not shaken by the loss of the King."

She talked on slowly, and her soft eyes seemed to be seeing pictures on the copper-hued ceiling. "I am grieving only for the people who trusted the King and believed in him."

"But aren't you grieving as a wife?"

"Why should I? Was he ever a husband to me? Have I ever heard his voice? Has he been anything but a symbol during all these past generations?"

"Then you have never been in love with him?" I asked. "Even when you married him?"

"That marriage," said Veeva, "is something I could never really understand. Did I ever tell you that I remembered a marriage ceremony?"

"You said it happened thousands of years ago, but—"

Shorty interrupted me. "But how could it?"

"That was an *earlier me—an earlier Queen Veeva*—one that I do not remember at all. I have only been told that it was me."

"Then you are not thousands of years old?" I asked.

"No."

"Betcha you're not a day over eighteen," said Shorty.

"I am supposed to be twenty-two thousand years old," said Veeva. "That was what the Firemakers told me when I was a little girl. They said I had been the Queen of the Ice through all those centuries, and that I would go on being Queen for thousands more years. But I know that this body of mine will die someday. And then—"

"You will keep on living?" Shorty asked.

"I'll be dead—as dead as anyone—all except my name. Some other little girl will become Queen Veeva, and the Firemakers will give her Whitey and teach her to ride, and she will learn to defend herself—"

"And to change voices into ice prisons?" Professor Peterson asked.

"That is not my doing," said Veeva. "It is one of Whitey's secrets. His intelligence is far greater than you realize. He can, in his own way, understand almost everything he hears. And when he wants to he can make sound—voices—freeze. I do not know how. His other power is his magical warmth. He is like these colorful walls that send out rays of light. But Whitey does not make light, he makes warmth—"

"Possibly electrical in some way," Peterson conjectured.

Lord Lorruth added his own comment. "I'm not sure that anyone will ever know just how the white tiger achieves this special miracle, but I'm convinced the animal has put his talent to good use. It was the rogues of my own party who failed to heed warnings and brought an icy death upon themselves trying to take advantage of the Queen."

"Is the tiger thousands of years old?" Shorty asked.

"No, he is simply the last of a unique species," said Veeva.

GANDL nodded. "When I was a small boy there were three such tigers, and there were stables for many more. I believe that this particular species came down through the ages as friends of our race, adapting to the ice and cold in the same way that our people had adapted."

"That is true," said Veeva. "We have had them for our pets all these twenty-two thousand years. That is a part of the Queen Veeva memories that were taught to me when I was young."

Her eyelids wavered and fell closed.

"She wants to sleep," I whispered. "We'd better leave her."

We drifted out to the great spacious corridor beyond the entrance. Shorty tried to be the last one out, but I herded him along to make sure he didn't linger. Then—

"Jim," Veeva called softly. "There's something I want to tell you."

My heart fairly leaped. I quickly turned and moved over to her bedside. She looked at me softly.

"I just wanted to thank you for—for catching me. I might have been killed... It's all coming back now. You carried me in here, didn't you?"

"With all my heart," I said, and I was suddenly bending down whispering to her, looking into her eyes, touching the side of her lovely face with my hand. "I've a thousand things to tell you, Veeva—"

"I have ten thousand years to listen, Jim," she said with a taunting laugh, "but your voice won't last that long."

I wondered what she meant by that. Perhaps she was telling me: "I am the Queen, and you are but one of countless men who will try to make love to me. But you can never be more than a passing amusement, a thing of the moment. My life will go on for thousands of years."

Yes, I thought, she was herself again, and now those honest revelations she had made while slightly out of her head were being forced into hiding.

"All right, live on for ten thousand years," I said in an almost irritated tone. "Live on a million years—it doesn't matter, because every minute of it I'll be madly in love with you."

I lifted her into my arms and kissed her. I have no way of describing just how passionately I kissed her, except to say I meant this to be a moment she wouldn't forget in a million years.

"You'd better go, Jim," she said.

As I walked away she was not laughing.

CHAPTER TWENTY-FIVE
A King Is Chosen

THE thousands of people who made up this kingdom were as interested as any public is in the affairs of its government and its leading personalities.

Their world was agog with excitement over the final passing of the old King. At first this overshadowed the other recent event—the strange death of the tall Firemaker.

But whereas the whole upheaval seemed to have been buried and covered over for keeps under the soft blanket of the memorial rituals, there was something under cover that wouldn't stay down. Namely, the personal convictions and ideals of one young rebel named Gandl.

Yes, all his mutterings in his sleep, planted there by my suggestions, had been accepted. Those sleepy words had been just coherent enough to explain why the King was scattered all over the floor and why his hand bones clung to a dagger that the dead Firemaker wore in his heart.

But Gandl had had a most rude awakening from that final dream session. His bewilderment at the entire situation had initially prevented him from expounding too much; but now, days later, the rumor was growing that Gandl privately denied his part in the affair.

"The King killed a Firemaker in defense of Gandl," was the persistent story throughout the kingdom. However, Gandl seemed to back off from confirming this notion. In fact he even began to belittle himself, saying he wasn't sure that the King had ever given him any messages at all. He always listened, as the King's Advisor should, but couldn't be certain he had ever heard anything.

The rumors troubled many people, especially those who believed that Gandl should have a chance to be King.

"The old King virtually placed the mantle upon him," they would argue. But for some reason Gandl still would not show interest in promoting the traditions. The Firemakers seemed more or less helpless. Some of them wanted to condemn him for blasphemies, but they were too afraid.

As for Gandl, his chief interest in life was to gather a little cluster of interested listeners around him and tell them about the outside world.

"There are many lands full of friendly people. There is sunshine half the time. There are no enemies waiting above our stairs. This is a myth that has been handed down by our forefathers from thousands of years back.

"The age of ice was upon our part of the world in those days. And our forefathers took refuge in the ice caverns to escape a hostile people.

"But that was long, long ago. The ice has moved away from those continents. It moved slowly, and we—our frightened forefathers—moved with it. And so here we are today, hundreds of generations later, still living underneath the ice and still afraid of enemies who forgot about us two hundred centuries ago."

IT was an impassioned appeal to face facts. It stirred the sluggish imaginations of many people.

One group after another would follow Gandl to the hallway where the row of dots had been cut in the wall like an endless border. Yes, they understood. Those dots represented years. The trail of time written there could be followed backward into past centuries.

And many would accompany Gandl on his tours into the remotest ends of the cave. There they would see ruins of the fine masonry and the engineering feats, which had once protected their race against falling ice. It was plain that their entrance into this land was a well-marked trail from the south.

"Gandl is right, I am convinced," Professor Peterson said one day. "The main stem of this race has come up from a temperate zone under the cover of ice. The occasional newcomers from the outside world—like ourselves—have given impetus to their arts of speech and use of tools."

But all of this was too baffling for most of the people. It called for too much thought and imagination and was hard to digest. And it made Gandl more than ever a subject of controversy.

However, Gandl was not seeking popularity. He was after the truth. He was much more eager to establish facts than to establish himself as King.

A new king was soon to be chosen. The air was full of rumors. But the days went by and no choice was announced.

I lost all track of time. But I knew it could not be long, now, until the ocean ice would start breaking and the *Aurora* would start back.

Lord Lorruth and Steve were continuing to make trips up to the surface, to convey sled-loads of the Lord's stored furs to Lady Lorruth. I wondered if her heart would thaw toward her husband...

"She has never found out he's still alive," Steve told me. "We take great precautions to get away before she or the captain can spot us. We essentially dump the furs and leave. But one day we bumped into Reuben Frabbel, and he told us she still has hopes of landing the captain's fortune—though he is usually too inebriated to realize her motives."

Steve and I were interrupted by a pair of messenger boys.

"Queen sends word to Pound. She let you take tiger sometimes to help carry furs. She wants see you."

"Me?" I asked hopefully. But no such luck.

"She wants see Pound."

I returned to my painting, and Steve went for a private interview with Veeva.

I was getting used to this. Various persons, including Shorty, Peterson, Lord Lorruth, Gandl, and the friendlier Firemakers, had been called aside by the Queen for interviews. I had been largely ignored, although Veeva had dropped by briefly a few times, but she had never paged me personally to come to her throne.

I WHILED away my time painting many scenes and portraits. She had provided me with equipment, including certain bright luminous paints quite new to me. She had requested that I do portraits of several of her friends—a Firemaker, a workman, a young mother, a digger from the mines, a few boys. And she would frequently stop at my private studio cavern to see how I was progressing.

"You're keeping me busy," I said, "to keep me out of mischief."

"You enjoy painting, don't you?"

"More than anything except making love to a beautiful Queen."

"How long will it take you to get your fill of painting down here?"

"I'll run out of paint first," I replied.

A short time after that, I was asked to come to a ceremony in the Red Room.

I was ushered to the stairway in the presence of the thousands of spectators, and then and there I was made King.

CHAPTER TWENTY-SIX
Lady Lucille Invades

IT WAS a coronation and a wedding ceremony, all in one, and I must say that I was more than a little amazed. My conduct throughout the occasion must have revealed my consternation. Afterward, Shorty told me he fully expected me to say, "This is so sudden!"

Well, it was sudden. For a Queen who was supposed to be twenty-two thousand years old it seemed like hurrying things up a bit not even to give her new King a five-minute warning before the wedding.

As a matter of fact I would have delighted in a little wooing—a few moonlight tiger rides and such—if I had known I stood a chance with her.

After the ceremony I learned that our match had been virtually sealed from the moment that I saved her from the balcony fall and kissed her.

But to make sure that her emotions weren't running away with her twenty-two thousand-year-old judgment, she had called in her various friends—and mine—to ask their opinions of me. Steve, Shorty, and the others must have done well by me.

At first the natives had advised her that I was essentially a fly-by-night outsider who would soon get homesick for my old world, and eventually desert.

"Consider the virtues of your former spouse," they had counseled. "How constant a partner he has been. In all these twenty-two thousand years he has never once tried to leave you."

"Nor to love me," she had replied.

But as these natives had watched me paint and had observed the interest I found in their faces and their manners of living, they had eventually revised their opinions.

And so I became the King. Not the *new* King or the *second* King—simply *the* King.

In the ceremony they assured me that I was twenty-two thousand and thirty years old, and that I would live forever. And, when I seemed a trifle confused over what I had done with my twenty-two thousand years of forgotten youth, they assured me that I had slept it away on an ornamental stone resting place.

Fortunately I remained apprehensive enough through the ceremony to hold back my smiles at the ridiculousness of it all. But it struck me funny to realize that, in a very real way, they now believed the former King's dusty old skeleton and me were one-and-the-same. This being the case, I had bashed the dead Firemaker with my own thighbone! The very thought gave me a catch in the side—or was it stitches?

"If you're gonna stay here and be King," Shorty said to me after the ceremony, "all I want is a job being janitor. I'll stick for life just to be around you and your good lookin' wife—if she'll promise not to make me walk that white lap-dog of hers."

Steve and Professor Peterson were also quick to congratulate me on my success; Gandl was a good sport too.

But I was not at all confident that I possessed the qualities of leadership I would need to serve as King. Most of the knotty problems would fall to Veeva and the Firemakers, as per tradition. But I must be ready when troubles were dumped into my lap.

Trouble came one day in the spring and its name was Lady Lucille Lorruth.

WITH the Frabbel brothers and Captain French as her escorts, Lady Lucille made the perilous hike over the glacier to our caverns.

When I came upon her she was firing a revolver at Veeva in the Red Room. Her escorts had waited on the long stairway. Lady Lucille, white-faced and wild-eyed with madness, had come to wreak revenge.

Each shot from her unsteady hand caused Veeva to dodge or leap for cover. The Queen—my wife—was at the mercy of a mad woman!

That was what I found as I rushed into the Red Room.

"Lady Lucille!" I cried. "Don't do it. Shoot at me, if you must. But not her."

Lady Lucille turned and gasped. "Jim McClurg! Come help me!"

"I'll help. Give me the gun!" I shouted, running toward her.

In answer she aimed at me and fired twice. I was half a room away, luckily, and she was an exceptionally bad shot.

The tiger bounded to Veeva's rescue in that moment, and the girl went riding straight toward this insane assailant.

"Don't!" I cried. "Don't go near—"

Veeva crossed like a streak of lightning, flashing her sword. Lady Lucille, tossing back her wild locks of streaked hair, aimed the pistol straight at her sworn enemy.

Click.

The gun was empty. Lady Lucille couldn't believe it. She was unprotected. The sword was coming. Her scream was inhuman.

Veeva flew past and gave a lightning-swift double stroke with her sharp weapon. Two wisps of hair jumped from the top of Lady Lucille's head.

Veeva spun around and raced back, twice, three times, four—and each time she took a deadly whack at her adversary's head, cropping the streaked hair closer, closer—

Lady Lucille emitted a blood-curdling moan and fell to the floor in a pitiful heap.

Veeva, panting but nevertheless laughing, looked down upon the vanquished foe. "Now that we understand each other, what can I do for you?"

Lady Lucille tried to defend herself by appealing to me. She accused Veeva of being everything from a husband stealer to a vampire; that her "curse" had demoralized the *Aurora's* crew and moreover had brought defeat upon Lord Lorruth and his party.

"You know I'm right, Jim McClurg." Lady Lucille, still crouched on the floor, beseeched me to back up her charges. "This awful woman wanted possession of my furs. And she has stolen my husband. He's hiding here—I know it. Reuben Frabbel told me."

"Lord Lorruth is here," I said, "but you can't see him. He doesn't owe you anything. He's given you the furs, literally out of the bigness of his heart—"

"That awful girl—"

"Silence," I snapped. "That 'girl' could teach you more loyalty than you ever dreamed. She's been faithful for years to a husband who has given her nothing. Your husband has given you everything—everything but his life, and you've wanted that too, so you'll be free to marry another man with another fortune!"

LADY LUCILLE'S eyes were wild, her lips twisted, but her words wouldn't come. She was stunned to silence by my angry broadside.

I sent some men up the stairs to get Captain French and the Frabbels, who had not been in the Red Room at the time of the scuffle, to take care of her.

The captain was at a loss, he said, over her terrible outbursts. In this instance her fury had been aroused over one of the furs—a fur skirt which Veeva herself had once received as a gift from Lord Lorruth and had decided to discard—ornamental bells and all—in her effort to keep back nothing that Lady Lucille might claim.

The ornamental bells were a part of a set, which Lord Lorruth had once purchased in Mexico, and their musical notes were identical in pitch. Some of them had been used on board the *Aurora,* and I remember that during my first sight of Veeva I had been struck by something familiar in the tinkling sounds of her ornaments.

For the present poor Lady Lorruth's fury was spent, and a sorry sight she was as the captain and the Frabbels led her away.

Within the hour Veeva sent Steve Pound forth with the white tiger to help the party get back safely to the ship—for the spring twilight had not prevented heavy snows and bitter weather.

The wisps of hair—blue-black, with a streak of white—became trophies in Veeva's collections.

"If I ever start being jealous, Jim, just show them to me and I promise to be good," Veeva laughed.

"You will never have any reason to be jealous," I promised.

CHAPTER TWENTY-SEVEN
Kindling Wood

I MUST record an event of tragedy before I bring this story to a close.

I am glad that I did not witness it. And I am especially glad that Veeva was not on the scene when it occurred.

Steve came back to us a few days after he had departed to escort Lady Lorruth and the rest of the party back to the brig.

I had doubted whether he would return to us. I knew he wanted to. Shorty had decided to stay. Professor Peterson was sure there was plenty of research waiting to keep him busy for a few years—perhaps for most of his life.

And Steve, loyal pal that he was, had wanted to see our new regime get off to a good start, and Veeva had promised to make him a Firemaker for as many years as he cared to stay. Gandl had assured him that there would be other arctic explorers before many years, now that steamboats were coming in.

But Steve was second in command on the *Aurora,* and his duty was plain.

And so he had taken his final leave when he and Whitey went forth to accompany the party to the ship. Whitey would of course return to us by himself.

As events turned out it was Steve who returned by himself.

"All the way back Lady Lorruth was like a frozen calm between storms," Steve related. "She rode the tiger with me because I made her. But I knew she was full of incoherent resentment. Now and then I'd drop her off and go back and help the others along. When we'd ride up to where she was waiting she wouldn't seem to see us, and she wouldn't speak. She'd just watch the tiger.

"I got to wondering if there was a spot between its eyes or something, the way she'd always be gazing there.

"Well, finally we plowed through the last mile of fog, so thick you could spread it like butter. The ice was breakin' and sliding along with the current, and there were some big dangerous bergs amongst the floes. I saw we were all fixed to weigh anchor and heave away, and it was high time.

"But Whitey was still standing there on the bank of ice, not knowing what to do. I was halfway up the ladder at the tailend of the party when I noticed. I went back and tried to make the tiger understand he was supposed to go home, and I pointed to the mountain ridge that you just could barely see through the thick mist.

"All at once she began shooting at us—Lady Lucille—standing up on the deck by herself. She had a rifle.

"By the time she'd shot three or four times I could make out the captain running down from the bridge yelling at her to stop. But she fired another shot—and that one did it."

STEVE POUND paused and drew a deep, long breath,

"Go on," said Shorty. "Tell us what happened."

But both Professor Peterson and Veeva knew what had happened.

"I didn't *hear* that last shot," said Steve, "because the sound froze into the biggest ball of ice you can imagine. One second there was the brig with sails ready to hoist on both masts, and the next second there was that great big ball of ice ten times the size of the ship. And all at once it was spinning over, because the side that had formed flat against the ice and water was lighter.

"There was an awful roar and clatter of ice crashin' against ice, and I knew the brig and everybody on it were doomed.

"Now it went floating down with the current—and then I turned to notice the awful thing that had happened to

Whitey. One of the bullets had got him through the shoulder. He was lying there in the snow, bleeding—dying."

Steve paused.

"Go on, please," said Veeva in a low voice that was almost a whisper.

"It musta—been that last bullet, I figure."

"What happened to the ship?" I asked. "It was built to stand a lot of pressure."

"It got battered into kindling wood," said Steve. "And it must have brought a sudden end to most everybody on board. I got a glimpse of Malonski floating along like a slab of ice. And I saw a few others. But no one but the captain made it to shore alive. He was nearly dead from a couple of terrible gashes; he lasted for about five minutes.

"Kind of glad I had those five minutes with him," Steve went on. "You see he'd managed to get to shore with someone in his arms—Lady Lucille. Yep, she was dead, and she was a pitiful looking thing, but it gave him kind of a last glow of pride, having me know he'd tried to save her.

"Well, that's it," said Steve, "and as soon as I get warmed up a bit I'll take a shovel and go back—"

"I'll take care of that," said Lord Lorruth quietly. And Gandl volunteered that he would get some boys and sleds and go along.

Poor Lady Lorruth. I often think of her and what a life of torture she made for herself. And when I get to thinking I always try to patch things up in a daydreamy sort of way. If I had just made more effort to show her that she was on the wrong track—

If some of us had understood her and helped her to talk out her troubles—

If—if—if—

If only we had somehow managed to bring her and Lord Lorruth together to help them patch up their difficulties, then perhaps…

But Steve Pound said he had tried that but Lord Lorruth was stubbornly determined not to visit with her. He had no intention of ever going back to her. And for five years past he had told himself that if she should ever sail north to find him he would remain hidden from her.

For Lord Lorruth was afraid of Lady Lucille, and Steve guessed there had been some narrow escapes from murder before this last fur-trading expedition.

And yet for all her faults and her madness, Lady Lucille Lorruth had had a share in reinventing the lives of several of us. Unintentionally, perhaps, but none the less true.

* * *

THE more years I spend in this strange sub-glacial world, the more I hope I live to be twenty thousand or so. That's the influence of Veeva and her traditions. Being King isn't a half-bad job when there's a beautiful Queen like Veeva.

Do I ever get homesick for the faraway world of tall buildings and rushing traffic and bright lights? Well, perhaps I do. Perhaps I'll send this account of my adventure back to the United States someday, just to keep contact with the busy surface world I used to know.

And if this should ever be printed, and should chance to be read by any of you who are contemplating a voyage into the Arctic, it carries an invitation to you to come down under the ice and see us.

Professor Peterson will have the world's most interesting lectures ready for you. And you'll want to get acquainted with Shorty and Steve and Lord Lorruth. You'll want to visit

Gandl, if he isn't off on a jaunt to Newfoundland or New York.

You'll want to meet Veeva, bless her heart, and all the family, bless their little hearts, and—well, anyhow drop in.

THE END

If you've enjoyed this book, you will not want to miss these terrific titles…

ARMCHAIR SCI-FI, FANTASY, & HORROR DOUBLE NOVELS, $12.95 each

D-1 **THE GALAXY RAIDERS** by William P. McGivern
SPACE STATION #1 by Frank Belknap Long

D-2 **THE PROGRAMMED PEOPLE** by Jack Sharkey
SLAVES OF THE CRYSTAL BRAIN by William Carter Sawtelle

D-3 **YOU'RE ALL ALONE** by Fritz Leiber
THE LIQUID MAN by Bernard C. Gilford

D-4 **CITADEL OF THE STAR LORDS** by Edmund Hamilton
VOYAGE TO ETERNITY by Milton Lesser

D-5 **IRON MEN OF VENUS** by Don Wilcox
THE MAN WITH ABSOLUTE MOTION by Noel Loomis

D-6 **WHO SOWS THE WIND...** by Rog Phillips
THE PUZZLE PLANET by Robert A. W. Lowndes

D-7 **PLANET OF DREAD** by Murray Leinster
TWICE UPON A TIME by Charles L. Fontenay

D-8 **THE TERROR OUT OF SPACE** by Dwight V. Swain
QUEST OF THE GOLDEN APE by Ivar Jorgensen and Adam Chase

D-9 **SECRET OF MARRACOTT DEEP** by Henry Slesar
PAWN OF THE BLACK FLEET by Mark Clifton.

D-10 **BEYOND THE RINGS OF SATURN** by Robert Moore Williams
A MAN OBSESSED by Alan E. Nourse

ARMCHAIR SCIENCE FICTION CLASSICS, $12.95 each

C-1 **THE GREEN MAN**
by Harold M. Sherman

C-2 **A TRACE OF MEMORY**
By Keith Laumer

C-3 **INTO PLUTONIAN DEPTHS**
by Stanton A. Coblentz

ARMCHAIR MASTERS OF SCIENCE FICTION SERIES, $16.95 each

M-1 **MASTERS OF SCIENCE FICTION, Vol. One**
Bryce Walton—"Dark of the Moon" and other tales

M-2 **MASTERS OF SCIENCE FICTION, Vol. Two**
Jerome Bixby—"One Way Street" and other tales

Made in the USA
Coppell, TX
04 February 2025

45431594R00127